Dangerous Company

Dangerous Company

DARK TALES
FROM TINSELTOWN

Peter Bart

miramax books

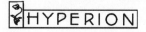

Contents

Dangerous Company

The Founder

The way I see it, I invented Starlight Terrace. Historians may not consider that a contribution to humanity, but it contributed a lot to "moi." Sure, there was something bogus about its origins, but this is Hollywood, after all; everything's a little on the bogus side.

When I first happened on Starlight Terrace, I was just resigning myself to the fact that I wouldn't step into the shoes of my role model, Zsa Zsa Gabor. So what was a middle-aged Hungarian yenta actress going to do? Take out a real estate license and hit the streets, that's what. One of those streets was a gorgeous little enclave nestled high in the Hollywood Hills that time had somehow passed by. There were a few neglected houses shrouded by a eucalyptus grove, but the neighborhood was virtually impossible to find and the street consisted of a maze of potholes. It was called Rattery Lane, which didn't exactly convey glitz and glamour.

So I decided that Rattery Lane had a future. I envisioned a secluded hideaway for stars and celebrities—a gated community with an aura of exclusivity. And it would be all mine—that is, I would lock up its business. Or at least try to.

All this was pretty ambitious given that I'd only just received my real estate license, becoming Eva Vaine & Associates (my real name was Eva Vajna, but Hungarian names don't look good on real estate signs). Changing my name was easier than changing the name of the street. After fruitless visits to the city council, I simply tore down the Rattery Lane signs and installed new ones saying Starlight Terrace, and I dropped a thousand bucks on the post office to pay attention. Bang—I had my Hollywood foothold!

Of course, there were some practical issues to deal with, like the existing residents. One was a plumber who dropped acid, had a jungle for a lawn and kept a decrepit camper in front of his house. I finally persuaded him to sell by telling him the city was installing a new sewer system through his front yard. I even hired a work crew for a day to start digging.

I placed ads in *Daily Variety* and got lucky when a talent manager named Marty Gellis decided to buy the plumber's place. Gellis was an old queen who had the kind of contacts that perfectly fit my plans. He basically tore down the house, creating a big white faux Tudor. Sure enough, Denise Turley, one of Marty's big-time clients, saw his house and I sold her a sprawling neo-Italianate place down the street on which she lavished well north of $500,000 for renovations. I sold another place to Eric Hoffman, a major macha at Warner Brothers, which was good because I wanted Starlight Terrace to attract the "suits" as well as the talent. Then came Elizabeth Donahue, who's in charge of daytime programming at the ABC network, and finally, I made my big score—Tom Patch. He was becoming one of the hottest young stars in town, and he put down $3 million for what was basically a tear-down.

Starlight Terrace was suddenly a hot address. I persuaded the residents to contribute to the installation of gates at the top and bottom of the winding street. Now the big realtors like Coldwell Banker—the guys who wouldn't even give an interview to a failed Hungarian actress—were knocking at my door, wanting to buy my company. "You're just the sort of visionary we need in our company," one guy tells me. He even offered me a scroll extolling my "leadership in real estate," but I told him where to put his scroll and that he was lucky it wasn't a plaque. I needed Coldwell Banker before, but I didn't need them now.

Besides, a company like that doesn't know how to do business with celebrities. When you're dealing with stars like Tom Patch or Denise Turley, you have to follow certain rules. First, you pacify their managers, their accountants and all their other functionaries so they don't get paranoid. You even hint they'll get a taste of the action. You deliberately place an absurdly high price on the property, knowing that each of these mavens will try negotiating you down. When the star finally shows up in person, you play it totally cool and you never, never "sell." If anything, you might even cite a few problems with the place—leaky faucets and an old furnace, that sort of stuff. When the talk gets to price, you go right back to the original number because you know that a star has no sense of money and will pay anything if he really wants the place.

Of course, none of this worked on my biggest deal on Starlight Terrace. The property in question—it was really a sort of mini-compound—sat at the top of the street and had a great view of Century City and the ocean. It was a fine old Spanish revival, maybe 9,000 square feet, and it was owned by a snooty couple named Penrose who had downtown banking connections—the sort of people who spent most of their time at their Newport Beach estate. I had tried to phone them several times but never got through, and my letters weren't answered either. I never understood what they were doing there to begin with; they belonged in Bel Air or in a fine old Hancock Park mansion. Then one day I was showing a house down the street when I saw an ambulance heading to the Penrose house. I did the old realtor trick, racing to the house and pretending to be part of the medical team. Anyway, Mr. Penrose had died of a heart attack, and within forty-eight hours I was showing the place to Barry Gal, and I was already nervous.

Gal was a good-looking guy who wore a black leather jacket and black jeans and had a vaguely Lebanese or Moroccan accent—he was from some place that was dangerous. When I told him the widow wanted $3 million, he immediately gave me six reasons why $2 million was the right number and that he would write a check immediately but would not negotiate. When I balked, he said something nice about my jewelry and pointed out that since he wasn't using a realtor, I might make a much bigger commission if I played ball. I got back to him the next morning, cutting the selling price from \$3 million to \$2.6 million, warning it would not go lower. Barry Gal responded by playing dirty: He sent two other realtors to visit the widow to cut me out. At the same time he sent me two dozen roses with a note saying, "Sorry about this, Zsa Zsa." We finally closed the deal at \$2.7 million and Barry promptly made a \$10,000 contribution to repainting the community gates. All right, I thought, maybe he wouldn't be so bad for Starlight Terrace after all.

Well, I was wrong. As things turned out, Barry Gal was to become the biggest pain in the ass Starlight Terrace had ever encountered. And I was blamed by the residents for bringing him in—a sort of "there goes the neighborhood" kind of thing. The whole experience made me realize that I had created something of a nightmare for myself in giving birth to Starlight Terrace. Sure, I'd made a lot of money by selling most of the homes, but when anything went bad, I got the phone calls. Why couldn't I get the city to put the streets in better shape? Why couldn't I improve garbage collection? Most important, why couldn't I get rid of Barry Gal?

Hell, I wasn't the mayor of Starlight Terrace. I'd dreamed it up, but that didn't mean its problems were my responsibility.

But then, Hollywood types are all spoiled. Since everyone always tells them they're perfect, they need someone to blame for their occasional imperfections. Even if that someone is merely a Hungarian yenta.

The Ghostwriter

It started on one of those Santa Ana days when scorching desert winds blast westward across the city and the air smells blow-torched. The relentless winds blow the smog offshore, giving Santa Monica Bay a vast yellow ring so it looks like a bathtub in desperate need of scrubbing. Los Angeles settles into an eerie lull when the Santa Anas blow, as though warning that earthquakes may rumble, fires may rage and people may seem vaguely psychotic. Before moving to L.A. twelve years ago, I read about Santa Ana days in Joan Didion's *Slouching Towards Bethlehem* and her words blew me away. I even tried to option her book for a client once, but she wanted too much money.

Though nothing good ever happens during Santa Ana time, something very good was about to happen to Sidney Garman, and I was to convey the news—a fact that pleased me greatly. As a new agent in the literary department of the

William Morris Agency, most of my time is spent telling people things they don't want to know. A studio has passed on their script. A director hates their rewrite and is pulling out of their movie. That is the usual grist of my daily rituals, but what I was about to tell Sidney Garman was quite different and I was stoked.

Especially for this client. Though not yet thirty, Sidney had been in a terrible funk during most of the three years I'd represented him, and I felt vaguely responsible. His was the classic case of the kid who walks into a casino, wins a million bucks and then can't ever get lucky again. At age twenty-four Sidney had struck pay dirt by selling his first screenplay for $1.2 million. It wasn't the usual action yarn; it was a textured, densely written father-son story about love and betrayal. It was made into a movie that received good reviews, did reasonable business and accounted for two Oscar nominations. More relevant, it won Sidney several high-paying assignments to write other scripts for important studio directors.

Not only had he failed on these jobs, but two other spec scripts of his also found no buyers. By the time I started representing him, he was locked in a textbook case of writer's block. He'd bought a huge house on Starlight Terrace, drove a Porsche and had a hot girlfriend, but he had nonetheless surrendered to his own failure. In his mind, he had grasped the brass ring and then stupidly, unforgivably, let it slip away.

Despite his hangdog, terminally depressed nature, I found myself liking Sidney. He was a gangly kid with fine features, an aquiline nose and haunted teal eyes who moved with an almost feline grace. He had made a pass at me two or three times, but we understood the unwritten rule. If I were to represent him effectively, our relationship had to be kept purely professional. Besides, he needed an analyst more than another quick fuck. He knew that and so did I.

Sauntering into my cramped office that morning, Sidney went through his habitual moves, leafing through the several books that I'd lately accumulated, scanning the cover pages of the scripts that lay across my desk, perusing the coverage provided by the office's freelance readers, never making eye contact, even after he slumped in the chair across from my desk. He ran his hand through his fine black hair, which looked badly in need of shampoo.

"It's gonna be too hot today," he finally mumbled. "Something's going to catch fire. Always does."

I decided to forge ahead. "Brace yourself, Sidney. I mean, really . . . Get it together."

Sidney stiffened. Finally, he made eye contact. "What's bugging you, Stacy?"

"Fox took your script off the market. They made a preemptive bid of 1.5 million dollars. It's take-it-or-leave-it time. I propose we take it."

"My script? . . . I don't get it . . ."

"Hello! We're talking about *Friends and Enemies*. Are you with me, Sidney? It went out last Friday to twelve places."

"A million . . . ?"

"A million five. Of the twelve people who saw it, eight expressed interest. I think we might still get other offers, but

Fox wants to close it out. The market for spec scripts is ice cold, Sidney. That's why I recommend—"

"*Friends and Enemies*! I don't fucking believe this! No fucking way . . ."

"Don't go into shock on me, Sidney. When I first saw it, I told you it's the best thing you've written since your first—"

"Best thing . . . Sure."

"So we have a business decision to make here. We take the offer or we go fishing for something bigger."

Sidney rose from his chair, as though facing reality for the first time. "I can't make that decision, Stacy. Not until I make a phone call."

"A phone call? Am I missing something here? Have you hired a business manager since I last saw you? A new agent, maybe?"

"Don't get paranoid on me, babe . . ."

"Okay. Then here's my phone. Make your call."

"It's a personal call."

I didn't like what I was hearing. "Tell me there's nothing weird going on here, Sidney. I mean, you *did* write the script, didn't you?"

"Of course I wrote the fucking script," Sidney shot back, but his face had a deer-in-the-headlights frozen stare. As he bolted from the office, he seemed to grunt. Or maybe it was a sob.

I was in a panic for the next hour. I called Sylvia Lear at Fox and told her I'd need some time before I could give her an answer. True to form, she threw a tantrum, telling me I had promised to take it off the market, that I was double-crossing her. I walked down the hall to talk to Mendel Kaplan, the chief of the agency's literary department who had anointed himself my mentor. Immensely fat with a huge swath of white hair, Mendel was the sort of agent who had long, pointless conversations with his clients, kibitzing about their investments and their golf scores. He also, I suspected, spent too much time talking to his own broker. When he finally hung up he signaled me into his office, which was four times the size of mine.

Mendel rose from his desk, stretched and scratched his balls. "Nasdaq is down eight points, the Internet stocks are crashing and I don't want to hear any more bad news," he said.

"What makes you think I have bad news?"

"You got the look on your face of someone who just found a cockroach in her matzo ball."

"Okay, I've got a problem. There's an offer of 1.5 million dollars on the table from Fox for a spec script. They want me to take it off the market."

"So take it off."

"The writer won't let me. He wants to think about it."

"Who's the writer?"

"Sidney Garman. He's ice cold—that's what's weird. Can't get arrested."

"Who does he think he is—Michael Fucking Crichton? Tell him to close."

"He's a weird kid—I don't think I can push him too hard."

"Look, the spec market is in the shitter. One and a half million is more than we've gotten for a script in months."

"I know, I know! Paramount had some interest, but they were talking eight hundred thousand, something like that."

"Look, Stacy, honey, I'm calling Fox. I'll tell them they got a deal. If this Garman kid gives you a hard time, blame it on me. Tell him our office got its signals mixed. I mean, this kid's been starving, right? Is he gonna sue or something?"

I nodded and retreated. There was a knot forming in the pit of my stomach. Mendel was old school. He didn't think twice about strong-arming a client. This was the William Morris office, after all. We always knew what was best for the client. Mendel also was under pressure to produce more revenue—that much I understood. Not enough writers were working and not enough material was moving.

Back in my office I was getting calls about another script. They were all passes. A producer from Warners wanted to know, "Are you hiding all the good stuff, Stacy? You're sending me shit." I hung up on him.

The calls kept coming, but nothing from Sidney. I couldn't focus. I sensed something had gone very wrong with Sidney Garman and his script, that somehow it would blow up in my face.

It was seven-thirty when I'd finally worked my way through my phone list. I was just emerging from the elevator when I saw Sidney standing in the lobby. He walked over, looking distracted.

"I want you to come with me, Stacy. There's someone you have to meet."

"I have a dinner at Morton's in an hour. I want to go home and take a shower."

Sidney just stared at me. "I need you, Stacy, okay? You always told me, 'if you need me real bad . . .' "

"Where is this guy I have to meet?"

"The Beverly Wilshire. He's at the bar. It's a two-minute walk."

The night was sweltering. People were moving in slow motion, undulating rather than walking, like creatures caught up in some sci-fi movie. I was sweating by the time I reached the hotel. The tall man standing at the far end of the long, burnished bar had that vaguely effete look of an artist who had fought many battles with both the muse and the bottle. His eyes sent out the message that he stood above the rules that governed other men. Shaking his hand, I instinctively disliked him.

"This is Sidney Garman," I heard Sidney Garman say. "This is my father."

"And that makes you . . . ?"

"I am Sidney Garman, Jr.," my client explained. "We have some things to explain, Stacy. I have assured my father that you are entirely trustworthy."

"To start with, maybe you could explain why you never used a 'Jr.' on your screenplays."

Sidney senior signaled the bartender. He was already nursing a scotch.

"I've been out of the business for twenty years," he said in a resonant voice that itself was a bit too mannered. His dark hair, streaked with gray, was combed straight back on his head and had the sort of laminated glisten normally imparted by hairdressers. "I suppose Sidney decided there was no need."

Sidney and I both ordered vodka and tonic. "Let me cut to the chase," Sidney junior said, his hand flicking away moisture from his forehead. "I didn't write the screenplay you sold today. My father did."

Reflexively, I looked over my shoulder to determine whether anyone could overhear us. "But the certificate of authorship . . . ," I protested. "There are documents."

"I know," Sidney senior replied.

"These things have to be corrected. I'll have to talk to our legal department. We could argue that this was an inadvertent—"

"We don't want to correct anything," Sidney senior announced, like a schoolmaster instructing an errant pupil. "We want the documents to say that Sidney wrote the script, not I. As far as the studios are concerned, this screenplay marks my son's return to form. It's his work."

I felt panic welling up. "And exactly what's the purpose of this deception? Is this some sort of exotic gift certificate?"

"No, this is a business decision," Sidney senior continued. "I am sixty-three years old. This town is run by young people who don't want to read something written by someone who is sixty-three years old, no less have meetings with him to discuss rewrites. Sidney has lots of friends around the studios. He understands the youth demo, as they call it. He talks the talk."

"And I can't write worth shit," Sidney junior interjected, taking a long drag on his vodka and tonic.

"My son seems to be down on himself. Surely a temporary

condition. He's a fine talent, you know. Did well at Yale. He was studying the classics. Really excelling . . ."

"Till I dropped out—"

"And the money goes to Sidney?" I cut in.

"You are an agent to the core," Sidney senior said with a patronizing smile that made my skin crawl. "My son and I have reached an understanding whereby the check goes to him. I will receive seventy-five percent of the earnings, he will receive twenty-five percent and you will, of course, commission the full amount."

"It's too risky," I said. "I won't go along with this. Besides, it's crazy. I mean, there are older writers working for the studios. There's Bill Goldman who wrote *Butch Cassidy*. There's . . ."

"Run out of names already, Stacy?" Sidney senior asked.

"Look, it's my dad's idea. These are his scripts and this is his plan," said Sidney junior.

"Scripts? You said scripts?"

"I am well into two other screenplays," said Sidney senior. "There will be an oeuvre."

I turned to Sidney junior. "And you are willing to march into Fox and represent yourself as the author of a screenplay that you had nothing to do with? You are willing to follow through with this deception?"

Sidney junior nodded. He squeezed the lime from his drink onto his tongue and winced with the sour taste.

"As my new agent, you might be curious about my screen-writing talents," Sidney senior said smoothly. "You're too young to remember, but I wrote and directed two films in the late 1960s, back when an artist could go out and make a movie without a big star and without special effects. My films did respectably, but they weren't hits. Then along came Spielberg and Lucas and suddenly all the movies had to be *Star Wars* or *Indiana Jones*. I had money. I moved to Paris. I stopped writing. I painted and traveled. Sidney's mother and I had divorced by then and I suppose it's safe to say that I enjoyed the company of beautiful women."

"He disappeared on us," Sidney junior said, "until last week."

"I tried to stay in touch. I sent letters and I sent money, but Sidney's mother tore up the letters and sent back the money."

The picture was crystallizing now. Sidney junior's big script sale six years earlier had dealt with father-son betrayal. It was a searing story of a son tracking down the father who'd abandoned him and wreaking revenge. The passion, and venom, of that story had fueled his movie and had marked the beginning, and end, of his career. He had never again been able to match his initial work.

"I know you're concerned about the risks," Sidney senior said. "I think we should let you think things over. If you are interested in working with us, I would urge you to call Fox and tell them the deal is closed at 1.5 million. If not, let us know by morning. Any questions?"

I glanced from father to son: the father, oleaginonsly handsome, setting forth his ultimatum; the son, wary but submissive, apparently willing to bury his anger. I briskly shook hands with them both and retreated from the bar.

Driving back to my place, I put the top down and felt my hair blow free in the hot night. I couldn't get over the notion that Junior didn't seem to understand what was overtaking him. He was in denial. On the other hand, that was a trait that I shared with him. I, too, was skilled at denying certain glaringly obvious facts.

Such as the fact that I was ten pounds overweight. Make that fifteen. Or the fact that I was a slob, my apartment in permanent disarray, my wardrobe in day-to-day crisis. I changed my bedding only when my boyfriend got on my case, which I forestalled by willingly sleeping on the wet spot. I was habitually late for appointments, even urgent ones. I was even fifteen minutes late for my annual "bonus meeting" at the agency, when my supervisor informed me how much I would make on top of my normal salary. All my life I had gotten away with things for fairly obvious reasons. My glibness. My ability to make people laugh. In a business of towering egos, I was skilled at self-mockery. I was not a threat to anyone, but when I was on my game I could persuade anyone to do anything. "You have brio," Mendel Kaplan once told me after I helped him re-sign a client who had already said yes to the shark agents over at CAA.

Of course, this gift of persuasion masked my own submissiveness. My shrink told me that because my father died when I was four, I was in perpetual need of male approval. Particularly older male approval, which accounted for two affairs with older men that dragged on far too long. My English professor in college looked alarmingly like Sidney Garman, Sr., replete with the smug self-confidence; he dumped me after six months. Perhaps I was presently overcompensating by having an affair with a twenty-two-year-old trainee at the agency who was preppie cute but terminally insecure.

I sometimes wondered whether I could ever have succeeded at anything other than agenting. Surely not on the same financial level. In a short time I had managed to build a stable of twenty-four clients, most of them writers, two of them young directors, all of them under the age of thirty-five. At an agency dominated by kvetchy old men, I was the enfant terrible who was in touch with what Mendel Kaplan called the "zitgeist." The studios were rabid in their pursuit of the "youth demo," and I controlled the writers who, in their eyes, held the keys to this kingdom. It's all bogus, since most of my clients detested the notion that they were "hot" because they were young or could "deliver" the young audience. Most hated their teen years and dreaded revisiting them, but that's where the big bucks resided.

It was bogus but it was working for me. With any luck at all my income would hit a million dollars within a couple of years. Mind you, I'd have no idea how to spend that kind of money, other than playing at Prada and Chanel or getting a bigger BMW. But money was what it was all about. I haggled for it all day long, and all around me at the office I heard the drone of voices insistently demanding one million dollars against ten or ten million dollars against five, the latter number representing percentages of net or gross receipts that will be due the star or director in the form of "contingent compensation." The mantra had turned the agency into a cathedral of money at which the clients came to worship.

The hot night had become soporific, and when I reached home I dozed off on the sofa, only to be awakened by a cold cloth on my forehead. I opened my eyes to see Ethan standing there, my boy lover.

"Are you all right, Stace? I heard you canceled dinner. You look like shit."

Hovering above me in the gloom, he was wearing only his white shirt and jockeys, and he looked alarmingly like Tom Cruise in *Risky Business*. This was no coincidence, it turned out, as he flicked on some music and started to dance the Tom Cruise dance, and despite myself I had to smile. "I'm sweaty and depressed," I shouted over the din, but that did not slow him down until the music ended and he came to rest on the sofa, one leg levitated above the other as in *Risky Business*.

"I told you I'm depressed! There's a crisis at the office."

He just stared back, flashing his lame post-preppie smile. One of his boy-toy games was to reenact love scenes from favorite past movies, and we had worked our way through *Belle de Jour* and *A Man and a Woman*, deftly bypassing *Last Tango in Paris*, until *Risky Business* confronted us. And Ethan was unrelenting.

"You're a hooker, remember?" Ethan said brightly. "You're Rebecca DeMornay, and it's not financially viable to say no to Tom."

I couldn't hold back laughter. "Come here, you pointy-pantsed little bastard," I called out to him.

At ten-fifteen the next morning Mendel Kaplan presided over a staff meeting of the literary department, reiterating the need to boost commissions.

"Wherever you look in this agency, the midlist clients are hurting us," Mendel declaimed in his nasal tones. "Whether actors, writers or directors, the midlist people cost more to service than they bring in. Painful though it may be, you've got to start peeling them off the client list. Those are the orders across every department of this agency. We want to sign the star writers and directors. We want the bright young comers. We don't want Mister In-between."

Even as Mendel was concluding his peroration, I could see Alan Sapirstein rolling his eyes in exasperation. A burly man in his fifties, Alan had been the key rival for Mendel's job and he made little effort to hide his disdain.

"Cut the shit, Mendel," Alan blurted. "You're instructing us to resign our older clients, which will land us right in the middle of an ageism class action suit. We can't do it, and besides, we shouldn't do it. It's wrong. That's a word you don't understand, Mendel, but it's wrong."

"I'm talking midlist, I'm not talking old," Mendel protested.

"Midlist, shmidlist. Did those dirtbags in Human Resources teach you that euphemism?" Alan snorted.

The debate was still raging when I snuck out to return to my office. I looked at the phone sheet. The first call of the day was from Sidney Garman. It didn't say "Sr." or "Jr.", but I could tell it wasn't Junior's number.

"The deal," Sidney senior said, his voice a little too unctuous. "Could you give me an update?"

"It's closed," I replied. "But once again, one of you has to sign the papers. With a deal this size, there will be lots of meetings with the development staff, with prospective directors. They may assign a producer. So you have to decide who provides the face time . . ."

"That's been decided," Sidney senior purred. "Relax. This isn't drug smuggling."

"No, but it's fraud. Your son is representing that he wrote a script that, in point of fact, you wrote. I could blow my career and he could blow his."

"He has no career," came the reply. "He's a one-story writer and he's told his story."

"And you were the principal character in that story."

"It was a work of fiction," Sidney senior said calmly. "I am meeting my son for lunch today. We will rehearse the initial meetings carefully. He will be well prepared."

"How do you know what they'll be asking?"

"I'm not suffering from Alzheimer's," he said. "I know the drill. It hasn't changed that much over the years."

As usual, Sidney senior's utter confidence grated on me.

"Don't assume they're a bunch of dumb kids," I cautioned. "They'll be firing off questions about character motivation, about structure. Arrogance can be very risky in this sort of situation."

I could hear Sidney senior take a breath.

"Listen to your own words, Stacy, and then tell me about arrogance. If I walked into that studio, those kids would be as dismissive of me as you are."

With that, Sidney senior hung up. I felt a surge of anger and stood up from my desk, but before I could go anywhere my assistant was muttering at me that two other clients were on the line and a third was waiting to see me. It was literally an hour later when I finally flung down my headset and fled the office for the quiet of the bathroom. By the time I returned to my office, my decision had been made. I canceled my lunch date and walked down to my car for the drive out to Sidney's house.

I had not been to his Starlight Terrace place since his enormous Halloween bash a year earlier. Sidney told me he'd spent $60,000 on food, booze and an extraordinary range of spooky special effects—skeletons rising from the garden, ghouls poking out of the chimneys, and so on. He had spared nothing and his three hundred guests relished his hospitality, which only he and I knew he couldn't really afford.

Sidney, I had long suspected, was turning into a sort of playboy prince. He had bought an eight-bedroom imitation French villa and had refurbished it, filling its rooms with French antiques and objets d'art. Only its third floor betrayed the true taste of its owner: The French motif abruptly ended as one climbed the stairs; up there it was a bachelor's wonderland of bright red walls, a state-of-the-art entertainment center, slot machines, a disco and built-in caves for fun and games.

Several months earlier, a lithe young wannabe actress named Deidre had become Sidney's live-in girlfriend, and it was she who answered the door, clad in a bikini that provided minimal coverage.

"Stacy . . . we didn't expect . . . We were just going for a swim."

"Sure . . ."

It seemed weird to follow a bikini-clad blonde through a darkened library filled with first editions. We found Sidney walking across the yard toward the pool, wearing jeans and his customary dazed expression. His hair was askew and he had a two-day stubble.

"What's happening?" Sidney asked.

"Let's sit down somewhere," I said. He led me to a cluster of well-upholstered chairs adjacent to the pool. Like everything else in the house they were top of the line, but desperately in need of cleaning. Deidre followed us.

"Look, I'm not famous for subtlety," I began. "You hate your father. You wrote a screenplay describing your hatred for your father."

"I suppose that's true."

"You suppose! What's to suppose?! If you hate this man, how are you going to spend the next weeks and months of your life impersonating him, defending his work before studio bureaucrats? What's wrong with you?"

"He wants to start over. A new relationship."

"And you trust him? He's a conceited narcissistic asshole, Sidney. You know it as well as I."

"Is she talking about your father?" Deidre put in. Sidney ignored her.

"What's worse," I said, "he's a fucking loser. What's he done all these years? He's floated around Europe, living off rich women. He's a world-class leech."

"He wrote a professional goddamn screenplay. That much you have to admit. I wish I'd written it."

"Who knows whether he wrote it?! For all we know he's got another writer stashed in Paris like he's got you stashed in L.A."

"Don't be ridiculous, Stacy. The guy's an artist . . ."

"He even looks like an artist," Deidre purred. "He's very good looking, for an older man."

"Think about what you're getting into, Sidney," I persisted. "The hassles with the studio, the fights with directors. You'll have to get your father to do rewrites. You'll have to cajole that son of a bitch into playing the game, not bolting off to Paris again."

Sidney was scrunching up his body, as was his habit when under assault. He looked like a child trying to get into the fetal position. Deidre was all over him, rubbing his back supportively. "Don't let her depress you, honey," she was cooing.

"Talk to me, Sidney," I implored.

Finally, there was momentary eye contact. "I'll lay it out for you, Stacy," he said. "I have no career. I can't write. You know that, I know that. I have no money left. I'm going to lose the house. This scam will get me back into the action. It will pay the mortgage. It may even get me a life . . ."

"*His* life!"

Sidney shrugged, got to his feet and, jeans and all, dove into the pool. He paddled around, facing away from me. I realized that our meeting was over. I headed for the front door. Deidre was tracking me. As I let myself out, I turned to her. "I had to give it a try," I said stupidly.

"You really are a bitch," said Deidre.

During the following weeks, my life seemed to career out of control. Arno Prokop, a brilliant young video director I had discovered, signed a deal with Warner Brothers to direct his first feature and promptly defected to Endeavor, a rival agency. My tensions with Mendel were rising, and instead of deflecting his criticism, I was foolishly fighting back. My mother decided to visit from Chicago in the midst of all this, continuing her habitual bad timing, and happened to meet Ethan.

"That young man . . . he's an assistant? A typist?" she inquired.

"We don't have typists anymore, Mom. He's my boyfriend. We don't have much in common. We don't talk much. He's for recreation."

"This job is making you coarse," my mother said.

"I was coarse before I got this job."

"Don't be coarse," she said. It was her favorite word.

Amid all this, the only thing that seemed to be going according to plan, incredibly, was the situation with the two Sidneys. Meetings had taken place between Sidney junior and three Fox development executives assigned to *Friends and Enemies*. According to the studio's project executive, Mark Colvin, the meetings had gone well. "Before putting it out to directors, it was important to strengthen the narrative arc, especially the third act," Colvin explained, in the customary "developmentese." Colvin had gone to Princeton and the Harvard Business School, but now, as a creative guru, he felt credentialed to fix any script and re-edit any movie. "The thing that impressed me was Sidney's flexibility, his willingness to listen," Colvin went on. "A few years ago he had a bad rep. He was difficult."

What Colvin didn't know, of course, was that Sidney could afford to be "flexible" because he wasn't going to be doing the rewrites. That would fall to Sidney senior. Even more surprising, father and son seemed to be bonding. Sidney senior was spending more and more time at his son's house on Starlight Terrace, hanging by the pool with Deidre. Now and then he would even borrow a laptop and do his writing in the library. The father was renting a cottage in Venice but never mentioned whether there was a woman in his life or whether he'd found friends.

Sidney senior knew I disliked him, or distrusted him, or both, and we rarely exchanged words. Once, when I'd called Sidney junior, Senior answered the phone instead. "I realize you think I'm some sort of interloper," he said, "but I would suggest you look at the results. My son is upbeat. He has money. It's all going well."

"So far, so good," I mumbled in retort.

"I think you should be aware that a second screenplay is ready for the marketplace," he said. "I think it is even better than the first."

"How did you write a new screenplay when you've been working on changes?"

"It was two-thirds done before I met you," he said. "It's more physical than *Friends and Enemies*. There's more action. It is called *Paths of Peril*."

I was dumbfounded. What I'd thought was a onetime accident was now threatening to become an ongoing drama. "I don't know what to say," was all I could muster.

"Happily your job is not to say. It is to sell. Good-bye."

The next day Sidney junior burst into my office, wide-eyed. "Oh, fuck . . ." was all he could say, as he slumped into a chair.

"What happened? Did Fox fire you?"

"The second script . . . It's even better . . . it's fucking great."

He plunked the screenplay atop the pile on my desk.

"I'm not sure I'm ready for round two yet."

"Do me a favor, Stacy. Read it tonight. Call me in the morning." He got up and practically flew out of my office.

I canceled a dinner with a business manager. He represented several important writers and knew I was desperate to sign them. "You must be on to a hot deal. Either that or you're in love. No, I take it back—it's a hot deal."

"Have it your way," I said. Ethan was petulant when he learned I would spend the evening with a script. We'd been bickering about our rituals of lovemaking. Our movie game had begun to grow old. The scenes he wanted to replicate basically had the girl doing all the work. Ethan argued this fit our personalities. "Boy-toy relationships never last longer than a couple of months," my friend Annie had warned me, and she was proving to be right.

Sidney junior, meanwhile, was also correct in his assessment. His father's second script was even sharper than his first. Reading it, I came to understand what the old guy was doing: He was imposing a classical approach to structure and character on contemporary subject matter. He had mastered the basic tools of the trade from the William Goldmans and Nunnally Johnsons of old, but weirdly, his head was anchored in today's world. While the dialogue scenes of the older writers tended to run to five or six pages, his were crisp.

Though it was eleven o'clock by the time I finished, I called Sidney junior to give him my reaction. "I can't believe what's happening," he said. "I'll call Dad."

He hung up, even as I realized that that was the first time he'd used the term "Dad." A few moments later my phone rang again. It was Sidney junior's voice, still breathless. "Dad is thrilled," he said. "He wants to have dinner tomorrow. The four of us. At Mr. Chow's. He wants to set things right."

"What things?"

"Eight P.M. Tomorrow." And he was gone again. There was something about the idea of dining with Senior and Junior together that gave me the creeps. Especially at Mr. Chow's, a restaurant that, for whatever reason, had become the industry gathering place after being deserted for over a decade. That was the point, I realized. Sidney senior felt the restaurant's fortunes reflected his own. Chow had made an amazing comeback. And now so had Sidney Garman, Sr.

The place was packed that next night. The ponytailed maitre d' looked at me like I was a discarded potsticker. I was twenty minutes late as usual. Sidney senior, elegant in black blazer and tan slacks, was seated at a prime table. Next to him was Deidre, ablaze in sequins, blond hair glistening, and then his son, clad in jeans and a ratty sports shirt. I assumed Sidney senior had dropped fifty bucks on the maitre d' because his table was wedged between Warren Beatty's and, on the other side, Barry Diller and Mike Nichols.

Father and son were cheerful, almost giddy. The tensions of earlier encounters seemed to have melted. I reported that I had already submitted *Paths of Peril* to twelve companies that morning, demanding that they give their answers within forty-eight hours. "I wanted to lend it a sense of urgency. I only submitted to people who had the authority to say 'buy' or 'pass.' No one else."

Sidney senior beamed as Deidre turned to him. "I'm proud of you," she said. "It's amazing."

"This place is full of industry people," I cautioned. "Let's be careful who says what to whom, if you get my drift."

Sidney junior nodded. He looked oddly fragile next to his father, who radiated a certain Old World panache in a room already over-heated with expansive egos. As I studied the adjoining tables Sidney senior started spinning stories of his favorite haunts in Paris, of the companions he'd hung out with and of his freewheeling jaunts to Ibiza, Sardinia and other pleasure spots. Deidre, in childlike fascination, was absorbing it all.

The waiter arrived and we ordered the usual Mr. Chow's exotica—seaweed, diced squab, drunken fish. I took advantage of the break in the conversation. "Tell me, Sidney, how did you make ends meet in Paris? You weren't writing screenplays yet . . . ?"

His gaze burrowed into me. "You're a very practical young woman, aren't you, Stacy?"

"I'm an agent. I spend my time making people's deals, finagling rewrite money, angling for more back-end points. I don't think great thoughts. I do people's fiscal laundry, wash their socks and underwear, that sort of thing."

"It seems to me you do these things very well."

"Thank you, Sidney. Now about Europe . . . the good life . . . ?"

"Odds and ends, really," he replied. "I did some translating. I wrote some articles. There were a couple of blacklisted American writers who were fed secret assignments from Hollywood but had forgotten how to write, so I was a sort of ghostwriter for the ghosts. I managed to make the acquaintance of beautiful and wealthy women. They are not in short supply in Paris, you know. It became too easy. So I decided to prove something to myself. Prove something even to my son."

Sidney junior was listening carefully now, and his father noticed.

"I tried to stay in touch, son, as I've told you before, but your mother made it impossible. And one day that very fine film you wrote came to Paris and I went to see it. That was really when I decided to sit down and do some writing. You inspired me, you might say. And having done so, I decided to come home."

"That's very touching," Deidre said. She dabbed away a tear.

"You were the heavy in that movie," I put in. "You don't deny that?" The food was being served now, however, and

Sidney senior was demonstrating to Deidre how to wrap her diced squab, applying some plum sauce, shredded scallions and other accoutrements and wrapping it all in a lettuce leaf. He had no intention of responding to my thrust. It occurred to me that, after only a month in Los Angeles, he seemed to blend in, chameleonlike. The rest of the room would see him as an older producer or director, a still attractive, if fading, roué. And Deidre was the admiring nymphet who was willingly accommodating the attentions of her mentor. It was his son who somehow seemed the odd man out.

"You okay, Sidney?" I inquired.

"Do you really think *Paths of Peril* will sell for the same kind of numbers as *Friends and Enemies*?" he asked.

"It wouldn't surprise me. It's a better piece. And there's a want-to-see out there for your work."

"I can't believe I'm gonna start a new round. People asking me what inspired me about these characters, probing what was in my head."

"But you're bringing it off. That's no small trick."

"Is this going to be my life, Stace? Impersonating my father? When I read his stuff . . . I mean, he's so goddamn facile. He's some piece of work."

"Remember, Sidney. It mustn't defeat you. It's got to get you writing again."

Junior jammed a dumpling into his mouth. He looked from his father to Deidre. "He seems to be inspiring *her*," Junior said with a scowl.

Paths of Peril had gone out to the market on Tuesday afternoon. By close of business Thursday we had four offers. The lowest was $1.2 million. The highest was $2.2 million. When Mendel heard about my latest auction, Sidney Garman was suddenly no longer my client alone. I was sharing him with Mendel Kaplan, and he was reporting details of the transaction to senior executives at the agency as well as leaking the news to *Daily Variety*. "Every deal has its own rhythm," he lectured me. "You've got to learn to feel the rhythm and respond."

"I already picked up the beat last time around," I snapped.

When *Daily Variety* reported the whirlwind round of bids the next morning, Warner Brothers hastily closed at $2.5 million. Not wanting to break the news on the phone, I arranged to meet father and son at Starlight Terrace. They were lunching beside the pool when I got there. A new housekeeper was serving salad niçoise replete with an expensive white wine. Sidney senior rose to greet me, kissing me on each cheek, pulling out my chair. Junior sat eating.

When I announced the price, Junior turned pale and rested his forehead against the table. Senior smiled broadly. "We'd better get you a new wardrobe, son," he said. "You're headed into a new orbit."

I explained the particulars of the deal. While the purchase price for *Friends and Enemies* had included a free rewrite, on *Paths of Peril*, the studio would have to pay another $500,000 for a set of changes, which undoubtedly would be mandated when a director and star became involved. Moreover, Sidney junior, as the author, would receive a deferment of another

$500,000 payable when the studio had recouped its print and advertising and production costs.

We finished off three bottles of wine that afternoon. Sidney senior took time to explain some of the options he had weighed in writing the scenario, predicting points a director might propose. By three-fifteen I excused myself.

I was at the front door when Senior overtook me. "You know, Stacy, I want you to improve a few deal points before you close."

"We're quite a ways down the road . . ."

"The deferment shouldn't be a flat five hundred thousand dollars. You know that as well as I. We should get ten percent of the gross. First-dollar gross, Stacy. I think you realize you made a bad deal, so fix it."

He turned abruptly and went back toward the pool. Driving back to the office, I was livid. This has-been was second-guessing me, demanding the sort of deal a Mel Gibson or a Tom Cruise would command. One thing was clear, Sidney junior was no longer my client; he had disappeared before my eyes. It was Sidney senior who would be calling the shots. It was going to be a whole new ride, and I had to decide whether I wanted to take it.

My discomfort increased at the morning staff meeting when the agency president, Rick Aaronoff, decided to single me out in one of his motivational speeches. Smarmily handsome at forty-two, Aaronoff reminded me of one of my mother's antique silver trays that had been polished so much it had lost its sheen. His gestures were too practiced, his suits too immaculate, but it all played well to the geezers who controlled the William Morris board of directors. To them, Aaronoff represented new blood. He was the face of change, and this morning, Aaronoff had decided that I, too, represented the future. "What Stacy Shuman has accomplished with Sidney Garman should be a model to all of us," he intoned. "She's taken a promising writer who was out of the business, and through her hard work she's given him a whole new career. She's given him 'mo.' What does 'mo' stand for, people?"

On cue, the agents around the huge table chanted "momentum." Rick Aaronoff seemed pleased, but he was just warming up. "What else does 'mo' stand for?"

"Motivation," came the answer from around the table.

"A star is reborn, thanks to Stacy," Aaronoff concluded. I could sense Mendel Kaplan shifting his position uneasily. He hated Aaronoff's motivational speeches. He said they reminded him of "warmed over Anthony Robbins." But there was no stopping him now. Aaronoff cited examples of stars and directors who had lately been down on their luck, imploring their agents to bring them back to life, to give them the double "mo." The growth of the William Morris Agency would come not just through signing new clients but also by nurturing existing ones. And I was the prime motivator this morning.

Eric Hoffman at Warner Brothers did not demonstrate as lofty an opinion of me as Rick Aaronoff when I phoned him that afternoon to renegotiate the deal on *Paths of Peril*. Hoffman, I knew, lived somewhere on Starlight Terrace, probably a few doors from Sidney Garman, Jr., but he displayed no neighborly empathy. While some business affairs functionaries were yellers and screamers, Hoffman had cultivated the art of understatement, conducting his negotiations in a sort of dry monotone. "Fucking outrageous," nonetheless was his response when I informed him I needed a gross participation, not a deferral, to close the deal.

"Look, my client is not someone off the street," I protested. "He knows the market."

"We're already paying him too much money up front."

"So I'll give you something back. I'll give you back two hundred fifty thousand dollars up front."

"Go fuck yourself, Stacy," Eric Hoffman responded softly.

"I'll give you five hundred thousand dollars. But I need more back end."

"I'll give you two and a half percent of the gross at breakeven."

"Ten percent from first dollar."

"I'll give you five percent. That's the end. Any other curveballs and the deal's down the shitter."

"Done."

I was astonished by my own negotiating prowess. Eric Hoffman was one of the toughest in the business. "With Eric, it's all payback and no giveback," was the way Mendel put it when I told him about the renegotiation. To Mendel, I had performed miracles.

Sidney Garman, Sr., did not agree. "You're cutting me back half a million bucks?" he stormed.

"If you want first-dollar gross, you've got to give something back. That's business. Writers don't get first-dollar gross."

"I don't like the deal."

"The deal is closed. You can either go back to the original or take what's on the table."

"I think you need to work on your negotiating skills." He hung up.

Sidney senior remained in a sour mood all week. He lit into his son for agreeing to an additional polish on *Friends and Enemies*. The studio felt that by expanding the woman's role, they might be able to attract Michelle Pfeiffer. To Sidney junior, this seemed reasonable; to his father, it diffused the story and would, in the end, require much more work than anyone had realized.

At the end of March I had to go to New York for a week. One of my writer clients had a play opening off-off-Broadway. The director was a bright young man whose movie had made a stir at Sundance, so I thought I'd hang with both of them. Ethan had some vacation time and he begged to come along. We stayed at the St. Regis and pigged out on room service.

When I got back to Los Angeles, an urgent message from Sidney junior greeted me. We had a drink at the same bar where I'd first met his father, except that it was only the two of us this time. The moment I saw him I knew something was awry. He'd lost weight and his clothes seemed to hang on him. There were dark circles under his eyes. There was so much work to do on both scripts, and a third was in preparation, he said, so his father felt it would be best for him to join his son on Starlight Terrace. Their disputes over the work were increasing, he confided. After every studio meeting Sidney senior would chastise him for not putting up more of a fight against the development executives.

"Michael Bay is ninety percent committed to direct *Paths of Peril*, but he says the script is too wordy," said Junior. "He says he wants me to physicalize more scenes—that's his word. He wants less dialogue, more action."

"So . . . ?"

"Except my father says it's a trap. He won't make the changes unless Michael Bay firmly commits."

"Doesn't he realize Bay's hot? *Pearl Harbor* made him a star."

" 'I won't audition for some fucking kid director.' That's what he says. I think you should come out and talk to him, Stacy. He needs a reality check. His ego is out of control."

My intuition about Sidney senior was to stay away. I knew the time would come when there would be a third script and the nightmare would be heightened. Yet my stock had soared at the agency because of Sidney Garman. Not only was my new bonus 30 percent higher than I'd anticipated, but they'd given me a $60,000 raise to boot. I was now considered a rising star at the agency, and Sidney Garman was the reason. I was getting "mo," as Rick Aaronoff reminded me. "I'm proud of you, kid," he reiterated at Mendel Kaplan's retirement party, making sure to pat me on the ass. "We're not choosing a successor to Mendel yet, but I'm telling you right now, you have a shot."

I'd put off my next meeting with Sidney senior as long as possible, but his calls had gotten more insistent, so I relented. The rain was pelting down when I got to Starlight Terrace. It seemed like half an hour before someone answered the bell at the house.

The door was finally opened by Sidney junior, who this time wore a clean shirt and tan slacks but seemed distanced as he led me to the library. "Can I get you some coffee?" I nodded and, to my surprise, he returned moments later with a cup of coffee, cream and sugar, but did not join me in the library, retreating instead to some other part of the house. I was putting all this together when Sidney senior, trailed by Deidre, entered the library. He looked regal in a navy blue smoking jacket and she was sexy in an exercise suit. Sidney junior returned now, and sat to one side.

"I'm glad you finally decided to pay us a visit," Sidney senior said. "I'd assumed you were so preoccupied with your new director clients that we writers were taking a backseat."

I'd expected a hassle, but not this early. "Writers are my first love," I said. "Besides, I've kept in touch."

An uneasy silence settled over the room. Deidre decided to break it. "Sidney found me a new trainer," she piped. "He puts me through a tough workout. Sidney's been doing it with me lately." By her body action, it was clear she was referring to Senior, not Junior. Indeed, she was sitting next to Senior, his hand resting on her thigh.

"How are the rewrites coming?" I asked.

"*Friends and Enemies* is ready for principal photography,"

Sidney senior said. "The cast is set. There are a few flurries over the budget but the studio has given it a green light, so those will pass." Noticing my coffee, he gave a signal to his son. "Some coffee, too," he said.

"And some Evian, please," Deidre added.

Junior vanished toward the kitchen. "I've been teaching my son to take a tougher line with the studio apparatchiks," Senior explained. "These are his contemporaries. They respond to toughness. Sidney is a tad too deferential."

"He understands the pecking order," I said supportively.

"He needs some of his father's testosterone," Deidre volunteered.

"If they want rewrites, they pay for them," Senior said. "The kids who are turning out spec scripts these days are a bunch of pussies. They've undermined the status of the writer."

Sidney junior returned to the library carrying a tray of coffee. He handed Deidre her Evian.

"A balance of terror has always existed in Hollywood," Sidney senior opined. "On one side were the Jack Warners, Harry Cohns and Darryl Zanucks, and on the other were the creative stalwarts, the artists. One side always tried to intimidate the other. That's why star directors were always being suspended in the old days. So were the Humphrey Bogarts and Clark Gables. It was all part of the terror. Today, the kids have let the studios assume too much control. And the agents have gone along with it."

"I don't agree with your thesis," I said. "Agents are the champions of the creatives. You should listen in on the battles . . ."

The phone rang and Sidney junior answered it, quietly assuring the caller that he would have to call him back. I noticed now that Deidre was holding Senior's hand. She was still the nymphet, but she now belonged to Sidney senior. If this was Senior's house, and these were Senior's scripts, then this was Senior's girl.

The conversation went on for about half an hour, before Senior announced that he had some work to do and Junior showed me to the door. I tried to make eye contact with him but he diverted his gaze.

"Good-bye, Stacy," he said simply. I kissed him on the cheek, but he did not respond. I might as well have kissed the butler.

Two days later I received the e-mail that I'd somehow expected. It was from Junior, but from the way it was written, I could tell it was the work of his father. "Having weighed the situation carefully, I have decided that Creative Artists Agency is better suited to represent my interests," the note said. "I thank you for your past efforts on my behalf and I know that you will have an immensely successful career. Thank you." It was signed Sidney Garman, Jr.

I should have been angry, but instead I was relieved. I had lost my appetite for Sidney Garman deals. I had also lost my appetite for Sidney Garman. For both Sidney Garmans. "Forget about 'em," Ethan said that night. "Unless you want to get someone to do a movie *about* 'em, not *by* 'em." Even as he was drilling away, it occurred to me to check whether Joan Didion might be interested in doing the script.

The Makeover

Marty Gellis hated waiting rooms and hated being kept waiting, but he understood that the waiting game was part of the business. Important people kept you waiting to remind you that they were important, and Brydon Foy was an important person. In the lexicon of the movie business, he was an A-list director. His last film had grossed $150 million in the United States alone. But Brydon had also become important to Marty because he had cast Denise Turley to play a supporting role in his new film, *Leviathan*. For the past two years, Marty had been trying without success to find a job for Denise, who'd been one of his long-standing clients. Though Marty was good at these things, he had run out of ways of explaining to her that fifty-two-year-old leading ladies were not in high demand in Hollywood. In Denise's mind, she was still a major star, and it was Marty, her manager, who had lost his clout.

Leviathan was in its third day of shooting when Marty got

the dreaded call, which led to instant sphincter arrest. "Brydon needs to see you at lunch break," said the assistant, in a small voice that triggered Marty's early warning system. No director takes time midshoot for a meeting like this unless there's a major problem, but what could have gone wrong after only three days, Marty wondered. Denise could be a royal pain in the ass, but even she understood what this role meant to her career. Surely she wouldn't self-destruct this quickly. Perhaps Brydon wanted to reduce her role or change her wardrobe, Marty reasoned, pacing Brydon's reception area. This was the sort of shit Marty was accustomed to dealing with. He was, after all, a personal manager. In the Hollywood hierarchy, it's the agents who find the projects, the lawyers who close the deals and the managers who dispense the Prozac to clients who hate their projects and disdain their deals. Such was his role in life. He was the humble facilitator, the faithful amanuensis.

The door to Brydon's office swung open now, and the tall, glowering director all but filled the space. Brydon was a big man with a deeply lined face that seemed at odds with his fine mane of blond hair, heavily streaked. His mannerisms were flamboyantly theatrical, and he used his flamboyance as a weapon of intimidation. Marty had learned that Brydon could seduce with his barbed wit or skewer with his sheer bitchiness, and it was he who set the mood. Marty felt himself wilting as Brydon beckoned him into his office.

"She's wrong for the role," Brydon brayed before Marty could even seat himself. "Casting Denise Turley was my worst idea since I tried dating girls in junior high school."

Okay, Marty thought, this is nightmare time. He was going to have to fight for his client; that was his job, but he had zero leverage. None at all. "Look, Brydon, you've been shooting for only three days," he said, irritated by his whiny tone. "This isn't like you. It's unprofessional. It's a rush to judgment. I mean, you're the ultimate pro, Brydon, and so is Denise . . ."

"Save the butter for a better occasion," Brydon snapped. "I've got to replace her. I have no choice."

"My God, you read her twice for the part. You even tested her, and a star of Denise's stature never agrees to test."

"You should have warned me, Marty, warned me about what she did to herself."

"What are you saying?"

"You know exactly what I'm saying. Sure I tested her—I admit all that. But when I told her the part was hers I didn't expect her to take a fucking Botox bath."

"She decided she needed a little face work," Marty protested.

"A little! We're not talking nips and tucks here. We're talking major makeover."

"But she looks great, right? I mean, she did it for the movie . . ."

"Look here, nebbish, I'm the director. I decide who looks great."

"She thought the character she's playing needed—"

"I need empathy from her. I need pathos. I tried to get a reaction shot from her this morning and she showed as much expression as Mount Rushmore. I can get more emotion shooting Grant's fucking tomb."

"We all know that in the first weeks after these procedures the facial muscles are a little stiff . . ."

"Hey, I like stiff—but not a stiff face. I want an actress, not a statue."

Marty knew he'd already lost the argument. It was lost the moment he'd walked into Brydon's office, but this was desperation time. He couldn't go back and tell Denise she'd been fired. It would destroy her. It would destroy him. He'd lose a client. And this was not a moment in his career when he could afford to lose a client. Times were getting tough. There were a lot of hot young managers out there who were nibbling at Marty's heels.

"I'm begging now, Brydon. We've known each other a long time. I'm begging for a second chance for her. Hear me out."

"What's to hear?" Brydon said. He was striding back and forth across his office, sweating. Marty had never seen Brydon sweat. He'd even whipped off the white scarf that he habitually kept draped around his shoulders. It was his signature scarf, which was actually a sort of mini-cape.

"You can talk to the writer, Brydon. You can talk back story. Denise's character had an automobile accident that required surgery. That's why her face—"

"You're reaching, Marty. It's beyond reaching."

"Hey, we're talking *Leviathan*, Brydon. This isn't *The Grapes of Wrath*. Your script was based on a fucking video game. It's not like you need Olivia de Havilland to bring off the part."

Brydon glared at him. "Now you're putting down my picture?"

"You're making a franchise picture. It's like they're already prepping the sequel."

"It's what today's kids want. I'm thinking commerce."

"So think commerce, Brydon. Denise is thinking commerce. I'm thinking commerce. But let's also think about the role . . ."

"The role needs a sensitive performance."

"Hey, I read the script. Denise is the mother of this Spider-Man sort of kid, and she turns out to be a manipulative bitch. Denise is a strong woman, Brydon. This is a perfect fit."

"You're rationalizing this to death. The mother cares for her son. She's afraid for him . . ."

"Care, shmare . . . it's from a fucking video game."

Brydon Foy was getting hot now. "Look, it's on my shoulders to make this damn thing work. There's a hundred million dollars riding on it. I've got to find a way of creating some reality. That's why I need actors, not refugees from some laser clinic."

Realizing that he'd been dismissed, Marty started for the door, then turned. "So I'll ask one favor. Only one. Will you give me that?"

"No."

"I want you to sleep on it. That's all. Then I want five minutes with you tomorrow before you start shooting."

"I don't have five minutes."

"Two minutes. Two minutes to save a career, for God's sake." Marty found himself getting teary. He knew he was pushing his luck.

"All right," Brydon snapped. "That's only 'cause you and I go back a long time, got it?"

"I love you, baby," Marty blurted, even as Brydon's door slammed in his face.

By the time Marty reached the parking lot, he was gasping for air. His asthma had been bothering him lately, and tension exacerbated the condition. He leaned against the fender of his Mercedes and took some deep breaths, or rather tried to. The noon sun felt like a blowtorch against his skin. Marty had treated himself to a sixtieth birthday facial peel six months earlier and his doctor had issued dire warnings to stay out of the sun. The image of his epidermis melting in the midday sun haunted his dreams.

Marty climbed into his car, started the engine and felt the initial rush of heat as the air conditioner clicked on. As he reviewed his options, his discomfort intensified. He could call Eric Hoffman, his neighbor on Starlight Terrace, and get his advice on the legal steps. After all, a deal's a deal. If the media got hold of this story the negative impact on Denise's career would be even greater. He would make the necessary calls, but first he had to deal with Denise. He reached for his cell phone, then pulled back. What could he tell her? If he told her the truth she would fly into one of her towering rages. Even a trivial call from a telemarketer could send Denise into a fury. An old-time director had once called Denise "an argument in search of an actress," and the line offended Marty, yet he understood what prompted it. Denise's fiery temper had worked for her during her halcyon years. Directors felt it added to her sex appeal, yet they knew her ego was lethal. Her co-stars, too, curbed their demands, fearful of Denise's lash.

In guiding his star client's career, Marty knew he held the trump card. "I can't go to Denise with that sort of demand," he would tell a studio chief. "You know Denise—she'll detonate." Denise's explosive temper indeed had empowered Marty to make Denise Turley more important than she really was.

But that was before the roles had started to fade away. By her early forties, it was clear from the scripts she was offered that Denise would no longer get the guy. One script even had her losing her boy toy and her dog.

For once in her life Denise Turley would now have to listen to the facts, unfiltered, uncompromised. Marty would be her reality check. She could accept it if she liked, or she could fire him if that struck her fancy. Marty had been at the management game for a very long time, and he was tired of taking the body blows for his clients and translating them into wet kisses.

As Marty pulled up at a light behind a row of cars, he reacted to the sound of a blaring horn coming from the curb. A black Mercedes was trying to pull in front of him. At the wheel was a smartly dressed fiftyish woman who was clearly an aggressive driver. And even now, as she gave him the finger, Marty realized she could be Denise Turley's twin. She wasn't waiting for him to capitulate and let her into line, she was just forging ahead, all but sideswiping Marty's car.

Marty felt a flash of road rage. He tried to swerve ahead, cutting her off before she could enter the flow of traffic. She jolted forward, coming to rest perhaps an inch from his fender. Now neither could move. It was a stalemate. "Rude motherfucker," the woman shouted.

"Learn some manners," Marty shouted.

"Go suck your dick," the woman shot back with such ferocity that Marty lapsed into stunned silence. This woman was easily as bad as Denise! Maybe even worse.

And then it struck him. There was a lesson here. Maybe even a strategy of last resort. It would probably fail, but everything else had failed. Of course, it would take some preparation. And some luck . . .

The horns were blaring behind him now. Marty had forgotten he was behind the wheel. He checked his watch. He would need to hurry if his scheme was going to be put into action. But first he would have to disengage from this harridan who was all but jutting into him.

Marty signaled the Range Rover that loomed behind him to let him back up a few feet, thus giving his adversary the space to maneuver her escape. Even as her black Mercedes bolted into traffic, she shouted a farewell epithet. Yes, he could visualize Denise in the driver's seat, relishing her victory.

Denise Turley had moved to her imposing neo-Italianate mansion on Starlight Terrace four years earlier when her third husband, a Swiss banker named Philippe, suddenly moved back to Europe. Her new home was four doors down from Marty's residence, a fact that did not exactly fill him with glee. Denise had first seen the place on her way to a dinner party at Marty's and had instantly fallen in love with it. As far as Marty was concerned, it was the ugliest house on Starlight Terrace; he also dreaded the notion of his most demanding client living in close proximity. Surely she would start summoning him at all hours of the night during her panic attacks.

In fact, Marty's fears were not realized. He'd drop by to see her once or twice a week to bring her scripts or otherwise listen to her complaints. Even her phone calls had been reduced to the point where Marty suspected she was talking to another personal manager. He had noticed a stranger slipping through her front gate on a few occasions, only to learn that he was yet another neighbor who lived atop the hill—one with whom Denise clearly was having a surreptitious affair. Marty yearned to know the identity of her secret lover, yet decided early on that the less he knew, the better.

Marty was admitted now by Denise's housekeeper, Dolly, a woman who, in Marty's estimation, possessed a saintly disposition to withstand her mistress's drumbeat of demands. Dolly was obviously curious about the satchel of camera gear that Marty was toting. "Miss Denise is not feeling happy today," she advised. "She's resting in her bedroom. I don't think she'll be ready to take some pictures."

"She won't even notice," Marty said. "I need a few minutes to set up in the den."

"I'm heating up some Nate 'n Al's chicken soup for Miss Denise," Dolly offered. "Like some?"

Denise's home, Marty felt, had all the intimacy of a Las Vegas hotel suite, with sterile white carpets, beige sofas and ornately framed paintings of English foxhunts. Though she commanded vivid views in all four directions, Denise kept her drapes drawn and her lights on almost all the time.

Once in the den, Marty dug into his bag to set up his video camera, which he directed at Denise's favorite chair. He adjusted the lights and removed a tall vase that interfered with the sight line.

Denise's piercing voice brought his fervid preparations to a halt. "You're an hour late, Marty," she said.

After all these years, her throaty summons still sent a chill through him. Actors who were trained for the stage all had big voices, Marty understood, but Denise's vocal powers seemed somehow more daunting. "Ignore me at your peril," her voice seemed to be saying.

"I came as fast as I could," he replied. "There was traffic."

She lit a cigarette and curled slowly into her chair, with the movements of a lethal snake. "So are you going to explain what's going on with my life?" she said. "I was scheduled to work today. This was supposed to be my third day."

Marty was relieved that she did not notice the video camera, which was rolling now. "Brydon saw the first day's dailies," he said, his voice flat. "He's decided you're wrong for the part."

"Bullshit."

"This is tough for me to tell you, Denise . . ."

"Bullshit."

"He read you for the role three months before the start of principal photography. He read you and he tested you and he hired you. Now, he says, because of your face work you look different."

"Of course I look different. Thank God, I look different."

"That's not the way he sees it. He says you're not giving him the reaction shots he needs. He feels your face isn't . . . isn't . . ."

"My face is fucking gorgeous. I look better than I did twenty years ago. And it cost me forty thousand fucking dollars to look this great."

"It's in the eye of the beholder."

"That faggot is trying to fire me 'cause I look too good! What does he know about how women should look?"

"That's not the issue, Denise. The issue is that he doesn't feel your look is right for the character."

"So faggots like sagging skin? They want droopy eyes? It's not like I'm Cher. I had a few tucks is all."

"Maybe you should have checked with him first, Denise. We'd talked about that . . ."

"It's none of his fucking business, Marty. It's my face. My career. We're not back in Bette Davis days when a leading lady could age gracefully. The cameramen back then knew how to protect their stars. They used screens and gels and fishnet gauze and diffused lighting. Today they blast the light at you and move in so tight the camera's practically in your twat."

"The business has changed, Denise. We have to accommodate it."

"Bullshit," Denise bellowed. "What planet is he living on? Even the fucking network news anchors have face work. And the guys—do you think Michael Douglas really looks like that?

Or fucking Pacino? Sly Stallone has had more work done than Joan Rivers. Forget just the faces—they're working butts and dicks."

Denise started to laugh. It was a shrill, mocking laugh, but it was a laugh nonetheless. Her eyes took fire, her nostrils flared and the cigarette she was smoking dropped out of her mouth as she laughed and clapped her hands.

Marty felt a surge of delight. This was Denise Turley at her petulant worst—and best. She looked outrageous, and theatrical. She was the actress from hell, and hence just what Brydon Foy deserved.

"If that's the way you feel, Denise, I will meet with Brydon tomorrow morning and convey your sentiments."

"Tell him I can play that fucking part better than anyone else he can get. If he wants to talk to other actresses in my age bracket, they've all had even more face work than I. He's going to see masks, not faces, but I can give him performance. I can give the part some sexual energy. Explain to him what sexual energy is, Marty."

Marty rose. "I shall deliver the message loud and clear."

Denise had started her grand exit when she saw Marty clicking off his video camera. "What the hell's that?" she barked. "I'm trying to save my career and you're shooting footage for *Lifestyles of the Rich and Famous*?"

"Don't worry about it," Marty said. He took out his handkerchief and dabbed his forehead as she swept out of the room. Then he packed up his camera and steeled himself for his next fateful encounter.

Brydon Foy was not happy. It was 7 A.M. and his lined face seemed like a road map of despair. The moment he saw Marty holding his cassette, he turned away. "I don't have any time," he protested. "I have to prepare the scene. My genius cinematographer can't figure out where to put the fucking camera."

"You promised me," Marty protested meekly. "The vid's only three minutes long. You promised me two minutes, so I need a minute of overtime."

"Do you realize there are over one hundred people in my crew waiting for me to tell them where to put their butts?"

"Three minutes. It will save you hours, long term. Three minutes. I'm begging . . ."

"I can't handle begging at seven in the morning," Brydon said as he trailed Marty into his dressing room. Marty said nothing as he stabbed the "start" button. Even as the tape started rolling, Marty saw Brydon stealing a glance at his script. Denise Turley's strident voice snapped him to attention. Suddenly Brydon was talking back to the tape. ". . . So I don't understand how women should look, right? . . . So I'm a fucking faggot and I don't know my craft . . . and I don't know how to light my actresses . . . Listen to the bitch . . . what a goddambitch . . ."

Marty watched his reactions with a mixture of panic and delight. "Forget what she's saying, Brydon. Look at her passion. How great she looks. The eyes, the mouth. The energy . . ."

"She thinks faggots can't direct women."

"That's just rhetoric, Brydon. You know Denise. But her look . . . the nuances of performance . . ."

"The bitch thinks I'd actually use her after that?"

"Think of the color she'll add to the character. The writer could throw her another scene, let her vent her outrage. She'll win an Oscar nomination . . ."

"I like her energy. I'll give you that," Brydon said, his bulky frame sinking into a chair.

"It's performance, Brydon," Marty bleated. "You're going to go and waste your time looking for another actress in the middle of your shoot when you can summon up this kind of performance?"

"Fuck you, Marty."

"What's that supposed to mean."

"You force me to see this insulting material? At seven in the morning I have to listen to insults!"

"Tell me you'll take her back, Brydon. Tell me you'll even give her more to do, maybe."

"You're really a deceitful son of a bitch, you know that?"

"I'm a manager. I have to give good deceit."

"You got balls. I'll give you that."

"And Denise?"

Brydon Foy got to his feet and headed for the door. "I'll think about it," he said, striding toward his set.

Marty was coughing again as he headed for his car. Another asthma attack. He needed some coffee, maybe even some lox and bagels at Hugo's. It had been a tough morning and he would treat himself to breakfast and the trades. Maybe that would calm his nerves.

He'd just bitten into his bagel when his cell phone sounded. It was Brydon's assistant. Denise Turley should report to the set as soon as possible, she said. She was needed in the first scene of the day.

When Marty told his client, Denise seemed more angry than pleased. "What's wrong with those people?" she said. "Stars don't snap to attention on a moment's notice. Tell 'em I'll be there by early afternoon."

"They'll wait for their star," Marty said, returning to his bagel. Suddenly he realized his asthma wasn't bothering him anymore.

Day of Reckoning

MEMO
To: Andrew Nathanson
From: Todd Plover

I have now completed the three meetings with my colleagues at the studio and am setting down herewith a record of what was said. I feel like a dork for having first resisted your suggestion of creating this record. Was I naïve? Sure I was. I'd convinced myself that the experience of making full disclosure to my colleagues would be reinforcing, that there would be hugs and pledges of support. And you, Andy, as my friend and attorney, were skeptical from the start. Your instincts were right. Maybe I've gotten too "touchy-feely" in my new manic need to put everything on the table. That's not to say, mind you, that I feel my position at the studio is in immediate jeopardy. It's just that—well, there was a subtext to the meetings that troubled me. Where I thought I'd get words of encouragement, instead I got veiled warnings. Reviewing it all, I feel that the nature of my relationship with my colleagues has irrevocably changed, though I can't quite define the nature of that change. Not yet, anyhow. Maybe it's too soon. Too much has happened too quickly. At the end of my meeting with Sara Shumway, my closest colleague, she even suggested sort of ominously that I take a few weeks off. "Go somewhere and get your head straight," is the way she put it. I told her I saw no need to do so, but at the end of this very long day, I think she may have a point.

At any rate, here is a record of my meetings as best I can recall them.

MEETING WITH SARA SHUMWAY, CO-PRESIDENT OF PRODUCTION

My first mistake was to start with Sara. Since she shares the top production slot with me and is openly gay, I felt she'd be empathetic. At least she seemed like a good warm-up for the meetings ahead. I was wrong.

Our session started at approximately ten-thirty. I'd followed her back to her office after our weekly production meeting. Sara was in her dress-down mode—sweater and jeans, and she was not having a good hair day. "So what did you want to chat about, Todd-o?" she asked.

"I'm meeting later with Linda and Nate," I explained. "So

I'd appreciate it if you would keep this conversation between us. I want to be the bearer of the news."

She'd been fiddling with her nails, but this brought her forward in her chair. "So spill it, kid. Did Fox make you a better offer?"

"It's not about career. It's about life. Lifestyle, actually."

"Okay, so you're converting to Catholicism. Or maybe Kabbalah?"

"Get serious, Sara."

She was standing in front of me, playfully grabbing the lapels of my jacket. "Come on, fess up, you anal preppie!"

I took a breath and blurted it out. "Sara, I am gay. I have moved out of my house. I have—"

"Slow down, Todd. You're the straightest person at this studio. Maybe in this whole fucking town. And now you're telling me . . ."

"Megan knows, of course. We're separating. No one else knows. No one except Steve."

"And Steve is . . . ?"

"I met him on the plane coming back from New York. He was sitting next to me actually."

". . . And you became instant asshole buddies? For once in my life I am speechless." Sara clamped her hand over her mouth and flung herself flat on the sofa.

"I love him. Steve, I mean. And rather than let my colleagues learn all this from the gossip mill . . . well, I wanted to tell you straight on."

"And why are you starting with me? 'Cause I'm an avowed

carpet-muncher you figured I'd give you a hug and a kiss and tell you, 'good boy, you're doing the right thing'?"

"Something like that."

"Holy shit," Sara said, subsiding again into stunned silence.

"I mean, if you're surprised, so am I. I'd never thought of myself as . . . ambiguous. Sexually, I mean. I'd never had an affair with a man. Never had fantasies about being gay. Never had a secret subscription to *Out* magazine."

"Hey, you don't need to persuade me. I'm good at picking up on these things."

"So I just want to let everyone know, and then get on with things. As far as I'm concerned, nothing is changed. I mean, it's a personal decision. It has no business ramifications."

Sara was standing in front of me again. "You're out of your fucking mind," she spat.

"What are you telling me?"

"Do you really think nothing will change? I mean, the Mister Straight of the studio suddenly announces he's a faggot, and that won't change the way the entire town deals with you? I should just give you the number of my shrink."

"Okay, so there's the shock factor. That I understand . . ."

"Let me tick off a few problems, Todd-o. Just in case you haven't thought this thing through . . ."

"Go ahead."

"Your wife, for example. Megan's got a lot of friends in this town. She's a beautiful woman of, what, thirty-seven . . . ?"

". . . Thirty-six."

". . . and there'll be lots of sympathy for her. I mean, I've always been a lesbo. I've never flown a different flag. But every wife in this town is going to rally to Megan's side and condemn you for faking her out."

"Okay, okay . . . I get it."

"And there's two other little things to consider. Like your job and my job. Just about every studio and network has one resident faggot. You know, just for show. But now our studio has co-presidents of production, both faggots. I mean, that goes beyond the corporate tolerance level. Stockholders may ask questions. Congressional witch-hunters may sense a conspiracy."

"I never figured you for paranoid, Sara."

"Not paranoid. Just real. When you've spent your entire life on the nether side of the street, you learn 'real.' "

"You're saying I'm jeopardizing your job?"

"And maybe yours."

"I think that's total bullshit. I don't believe the parent company gives a goddamn who I get into bed with at night."

"You've been listening to too many of those 'diversity' speeches, kiddo. You're believing the Human Resources propaganda."

"So what would you have me do, Sara? It's obvious you totally disapprove . . ."

"Go away for a few days. Think this through. Put Steve back on the plane. You're getting in way over your head."

"Thanks for the advice, Sara. You won't take it personally if I ignore it?"

"And you won't take it personally that I've given it?"

Sara gave me a quick kiss on the cheek. "I'm sorry, kid. I know you wanted me to say all sorts of warm-and-runny things, and I've failed you. I'm not much of a feel-good faggot is the problem."

"I got that message."

"So what the fuck . . ."

As I left her office, I saw her staring glumly out the window. She had thoroughly depressed me, and I felt I had had the same effect on her. This was not going to be an easy day.

I checked my watch: 10:45. Time for my second meeting. Time to take on Linda Laurence.

MEETING WITH LINDA LAURENCE, CHAIR OF THE STUDIO

In view of my complicated talk with Sara, I decided to get right down to business at my second meeting. As chairman of the studio, Linda Laurence has final authority over what movies are made as well as all staffing issues. If my future were in question, as Sara seemed to think, then it would ultimately be up to Linda, who I know to be a very empathetic and liberal person.

"The production meeting this morning was very constructive," Linda said as I entered her vast office. "I'm glad we finally put *Faraway Islands* into turnaround. The budget was crazy—"

"I need to talk to you about a personal issue," I interrupted.

"My marriage to Megan is over. I have moved into a new place. A new place with a new lover. His name is Steve . . ."

"Steve is a 'he'?"

"I'm a gay person, Linda. I want you to know."

She stared at me, wide-eyed. "Run that by me one more time."

"I'm living with a guy."

"Oh, shit."

"Exactly."

"And Megan. I mean, she and I weren't close, but . . . how is she taking it?"

"Badly, I'm afraid. Lots of tears. Cries of betrayal. That sort of thing."

"My goodness," Linda said, hand on her forehead.

"I feel very bad about that, but good about other things. There was a part of my being that had been asleep for years. I don't know how to explain it. I feel bad for Megan, but I also feel very much alive for the first time in a very long time."

"Well, you know how I feel about these things, Todd. I mean, I'm open to any lifestyle. I am not a judgmental person. You know that about me."

"I do. You are a very feeling person."

I saw Linda reach for the telephone. I could hardly believe what she was doing. She was summoning the chief of Human Resources to her office. It was like she was embracing me and at the same time summoning the death squad.

"Do we really have to have Karla here for this?" I protested.

Linda flushed. Clearly, she was embarrassed by her own action. "It's not about you, it's about me. You know the way I am. I say what I think, but I don't want to say something that's inappropriate. I mean, I want to be supportive, Todd, but I don't want to put my foot in it . . . Corporately, I mean."

"There's a reason the staff calls her Karla Buchenwald," I said.

"Someone in her position . . . Karla Birkenwell's, I mean . . . she's in a difficult spot. She has corporate responsibilities. You understand."

"I'm afraid I don't."

Karla strode into the office. As usual, she was steely-faced and all business.

"Karla, Todd and I are having a personal chat," Linda said. "But there may be aspects of it . . . well, I thought you should be in on it. Todd understands."

"What's the issue here?" Karla asked.

"Todd has left his wife. He has just told me that he's decided he is gay. Is that the gist of it, Todd?"

"Yes, it is."

"And I explained that Todd's personal life is his own affair. I am very nonjudgmental about these things, as everyone in the industry knows. My husband and I were co-chairs of the Gay Rights celebration only a month ago."

"Your diversity record speaks for itself," Karla said.

I sensed this was the time for me to read something into the record. "I just want you both to know that I am fully committed to my work," I said. "I don't plan to take my eye off the ball. I appreciate the responsibilities you have given me, Linda, and I won't let you down."

"I know you won't," Linda said. "But I must ask . . . it's a stupid question, I suppose. But have you known about this . . . condition for long? Your being gay, I mean?"

"You don't have to respond to that," Karla said sharply.

"No, I'll be glad to respond. I'd never thought of myself as gay. This whole thing took me by surprise. I mean, I suddenly realized that I was in love. Really in love."

"With Steve? I mean, you are having sex with Steve?"

Karla sat forward. "You don't have to answer that," she said again.

"Yes, we're having sex. Best sex I've ever had."

Linda was getting twitchy. "Well, I just want you to be happy. I also want Megan to be happy. I suppose I should call her. Would that be okay, Todd?"

"Certainly . . ."

Linda looked over at Karla. "There would be nothing wrong . . . ?"

"Not at all. On the other hand, Todd, there are certain issues that we should address. Business issues."

"Like . . . ?"

"Like who is your domestic partner? Your insurance covers one significant other. Your new . . . friend . . ."

". . . Steve . . ."

"He is not covered. Not unless you request a change, and that, too, has ramifications . . ."

"I'm afraid I'm not really ready to deal with that sort of thing," I said.

"You've made decisions. They will lead to other decisions."

"Karla has a point," Linda Laurence said.

"There is also the question of public relations," Karla said. "The press, I mean . . ."

I felt a rush of anger. "What are you telling me? Do you want to plant an item in the gossip columns to protect the corporation?"

"I'm sure Todd doesn't want publicity," Linda put in quickly.

"Word will get out," Karla said. "If you want to control the story, then you must arrange the right placement. Otherwise there will be nasty gossip in the trades. It could hurt the corporation."

"Karla has a point," Linda said.

"I can't deal with this," I protested. "I'm not ready . . ."

"You were ready to move in with 'Steve,' " Karla said. "One action precipitates another."

"Todd needs time to digest all of this," Linda said. "I mean, these are lifestyle questions, not corporate questions, Karla."

"But they will cause corporate problems unless we are proactive," Karla responded. "It's my job to be proactive."

Karla got to her feet. "You and I should spend some time tomorrow," she said to me.

"Meaning what? Does the corporation want me to take a

physical? Are you worried my disease will prove contagious?"

Karla stared at me, then wheeled and left the office. Linda was clearly discomfited. "We all want the best for you, Todd. You know that, don't you?"

"I guess so . . ."

"Whatever lifestyle suits you, that's fine by me. You know that, too?"

I nodded.

"Only a couple of months ago my husband and I were co-chairs of the Gay Rights . . . But I told you that, didn't I?"

I nodded again.

"It's just that this is a bit of a shock. I mean, you feel you know someone, and then it turns out otherwise."

"I guess I didn't even know myself."

"But of course, you're still the same person . . ."

"I'm not. Not really. I'm the same person, but I'm a gay person, and that's quite a different person."

Linda was staring at me again, quizzically. Then she walked over to me and gave me a kiss. It was not the sort of kiss you get at parties or premieres. It was a real kiss. A wet one. There were tears, too.

Then I realized they were my tears.

Which brings me to my final meeting.

MEETING WITH NATHAN STROM, EXECUTIVE VICE PRESIDENT, BUSINESS AFFAIRS

Nate Strom is the studio's business guru. His power, of course, is equal to that of Linda Laurence's. And though I've worked with him for seven years, he still scares me shitless with his intellect and his fierce stare.

The meeting with Nate Strom was the one I most feared, but I was wrong. From the moment I walked into his office, Strom made it easy. He held up his hand before I could even say "good morning." He said, "Look, kid, I know why you're here. I've heard the sob story, okay? So let me say the following: Who gives a shit? I don't care if you're fucking a cage full of monkeys, just give me some hit movies. That's all I have to say."

"I get the message."

"So can I give you some advice? I mean, is that why you're making the rounds with your sorry tale?"

"I just wanted to tell my friends at the studio what's happened so that they don't hear—"

"Stop right there. You don't have any friends at the studio. None of us has any friends at the studio. When the pictures are hitting and the numbers are right, we all are buddies, understand? When things go south, forget it."

"What are you really telling me, Nate?"

"I'm telling you to get back to your office and get to work like nothing ever happened. Don't have any more meetings, don't confide any more information about your personal life, don't talk to any reporters . . ."

"Karla Buchenwald wants to meet with me about a possible press release."

"Who gives a shit what Karla wants? She's an automaton. She talks, no one listens."

"So you're telling me to shut up."

"That's my message. This town is full of gays in positions of power. Some are in the closet, some are out. Does anyone give a shit?"

"I suppose not."

"So why carry on about your so-called lifestyle change? Why rub it into people's faces? Look, you made your rep here by developing three of the best action pictures of the decade. You gave the careers of Schwarzenegger and Stallone an injection of testosterone. This town thinks of you in terms of high body counts and big grosses. That's all we want to know. We don't care who you sleep with or who's on top."

"I get the message, Nate. Thank you for giving it to me straight."

Nate Strom grinned. "See, there's still nothing wrong with straight. Sometimes, that is."

Nate crossed the room, fiddling with the ceramic cigarette he sucks on in an effort to quit smoking. "So let's get the Megan business out of the way. How big a problem is she going to be?"

"Plenty big."

"The classic betrayed wife syndrome? That's always trouble."

"We haven't been getting on for a couple of years."

"That's not news to me."

"What do you mean?"

"Look, I'd play it tough with her. Let your lawyer do the talking. Offer a deal, but don't get into any sidebar agreements."

"You said it wasn't news to you that Megan and I . . . ?"

"Hey, get real, kid. There were rumors . . ."

"Rumors? About me? But I never did anything. I never strayed."

"Rumors about your wife. You know what I'm talking about."

"Hey, I'm in the dark."

"Your wife and Sara Shumway. I mean, it's all over the studio."

"Are you telling me that Megan and Sara were having an affair?"

"No, I'm giving you the gossip. Did I see them in bed together? No. I watch the numbers, Todd, not the bedrooms."

"Megan isn't a lesbian. That's the dumbest thing . . ."

"So maybe Sara was giving her lessons. How the hell should I know? I'm just telling you this because it may help you make your deal. Let's say the gossip is true, so that's an area of vulnerability, right? You press a little, she gives a little. The endgame, Todd, is to make a quick deal. The worst thing for you would be a long and ugly public battle. That's something you don't need."

"I hear you."

Nate Strom put his hands on my shoulders. I smelled his cigarette breath as he talked—the fake ciggies weren't doing their job. "Look, kid, I'm trying to help, got it? You may be getting a lot of lip service from the others, but I'm a bottom line kind of guy and I'm trying to give you some bottom line kind of help. I want you to come out of this intact. You're a good kid, and like I said before, I don't give a shit who you're fucking or why."

"Thank you, Nate. You're a friend."

"No, kid, but I'll pass for an ally."

So that's pretty much the saga, Andy. Now that I've reviewed it all in my mind I feel pretty good about things on one level. I don't think I'm about to be fired. I don't think my colleagues will spurn me. On the other hand, I've naïvely underestimated the impact of my actions. I realize I'm behaving like a self-involved college sophomore. I've lost my perspective on the world around me. I can fix that, Andy, given a little time. I've just got to follow Nate Strom's advice and get back to work. I've got to prove to my colleagues and to the town that I haven't lost my focus.

Incidentally, I got a call from Megan tonight in the midst of dictating all this. It seems she wants to bring over our cat; in the rush of events she'd forgotten about him. While I had her on the phone, I asked her whether she was really having an affair with Sara Shumway.

Guess what: She hung up on me, Andy.

The Neighbors I

Todd Plover was cold. He also had a cold, and he resented both conditions as he trundled along the dark, pitted road. He was late for the meeting, but he still picked his steps cautiously, mindful of the potholes that lay in his path and also of his own catatonic clumsiness. All his life Todd had been embarrassed by his pratfalls; he'd even tumbled at his own wedding. His bride, Megan, had thought she was marrying someone sleekly athletic. She'd ultimately come to understand that Todd was the opposite of everything he appeared to be.

And now on this blustery, moonless night, he was utterly miserable finding himself trekking down Starlight Terrace for a meeting he desperately did not want to attend. He was president of a neighborhood association when he no longer even lived in the neighborhood, but he could not confide that secret to anyone at the meeting. As far as they were concerned, he still resided with his wife, Megan, at 1884 Starlight

Terrace, though five days earlier he had, in fact, moved to a loft at Venice Beach. But he had told no one and Megan had agreed to their vow of silence, at least until he could alert colleagues at work.

Todd cursed as he stumbled again on a loose rock, catching his fall, surprised that for once he didn't land on his ass—probably because no one was around to witness. He wished now he had parked in Denise Turley's driveway, but he had decided to preserve secrecy by parking in front of his own house and making his way down the street to avoid the neighbors' scrutiny. It was a dumb decision that had made him even later for the meeting, while endangering his well-being and aggravating his cold.

Denise's front gate loomed ahead now as Todd evaded another hole. How could they have let their streets get so dilapidated, he wondered, knowing, of course, that he and his neighbors had regularly complained to the City of Los Angeles without result. No doubt the issue would be brought up anew at the meeting tonight, along with other complaints relating to life in the Hollywood Hills.

Todd had never been comfortable in his role as neighborhood custodian. The previous president, Eric Hoffman, had pressed him into service. Hoffman was an important executive at Warner Brothers and Todd, as co-president of production at a rival studio, did not want to offend an industry colleague. At thirty-six, Todd was, in fact, the youngest film industry player to hold that lofty title, and as such he was sensitive to his civic responsibilities.

In fact, he felt hypersensitive these days about virtually everything. Todd sensed his life was whirling out of control, yet he knew that to friends and colleagues he personified control and moderation. That had always been his calling card. Even his mother had always described him as "the responsible one." If only she had heard Megan screaming at him that previous night. "You don't understand the meaning of the word 'responsibility,' " was her clarion call.

A cold rain had begun to fall as Todd hurried through Denise Turley's rococo gate, which shielded her neo-Italianate mansion. He was poised to press the door button, which resided on the nose of a brass ocelot, when the door suddenly swung open. Blinking against the sudden onslaught of light, Todd recognized the smiling face of Dolly, who had long been Denise Turley's housekeeper and amanuensis. "The others are already here, Mr. Todd," Dolly said. "And Miss Denise will be down shortly."

Todd had been in Denise Turley's house once before, and he remembered its mixed messages. The living room resembled the suite of a Las Vegas high roller. Todd knew that Denise had served her time as a Vegas showgirl before becoming a major star. Her "discovery," Todd had been told, had been hastened by a torrid affair with her first director.

The meetings of the Starlight Terrace Neighborhood Association alternated from house to house, and this month it was Denise Turley's turn to play hostess, though she had rarely attended prior meetings. Entering the living room, Todd saw that most of the other association directors were in attendance. They were a disparate lot, and upon becoming president, Todd quickly realized they agreed on almost nothing, yet were good-natured in their differences. Marty Gellis, a silver-haired talent manager, wore a habitual pained expression, as though he were about to pass a kidney stone. Sidney Garman, a screenwriter even younger than Todd, looked like he hadn't slept for days, and also hadn't shaved. By contrast, both Eric Hoffman from Warner Brothers and Elizabeth Donahue from the ABC network were important players at their respective companies, but while Hoffman fitted the role of the "suit," Donahue struck Todd as being relentlessly edgy and unpredictable. Todd never could figure out exactly what Nancy Mendoza did for a living, but felt she seemed too straight for Starlight Terrace with her prim Talbots wardrobe and severe hairstyle. And then there was Tom Patch, looking fit and relaxed in his form-fitting T-shirt and jeans, hair slicked back, carefully cultivating, to Todd's perspective, the "look" of a budding superstar.

Todd also was surprised to recognize Eva Vaine, the realtor who'd sold all of them their houses but who rarely deigned to attend neighborhood meetings. Eva was, as usual, a fashion statement with her poof of teased blond hair and wearing a nubby bright red wool suit that seemed to shout "Chanel."

Todd moved among them, shaking hands, exchanging small talk even as Dolly circulated with a tray of seafood hors d'oeuvres. "Miss Denise will be right down any moment," she reiterated patiently to each guest.

"Denise likes dramatic entrances, as you all know," said

Marty Gellis, plucking a second shrimp from Dolly's tray. "I should know. I've represented her for twenty years."

"Seems I'm not doing much better when it comes to punctuality," Todd said apologetically. "Should we get started straight away?"

"While we were waiting, Elizabeth reminded us that two years have passed since the city agreed to put speed bumps on our street, yet nothing's been done," Eric Hoffman said in his measured, lawyerly cadence.

"Speed bumps? The whole street is a speed bump," said Marty Gellis. "The city should repave the neighborhood."

"Garbage collection also was raised," Hoffman continued. "Nancy Mendoza points out that the collection days have shifted from Thursday to Friday, then back to Thursday again." Todd had started taking notes while stifling a sneeze.

"Forgive me if I sound like the voice of the *National Enquirer*, but can't we dish about Barry Gal before dealing with the boring stuff?" said Sidney Garman. "I mean, when's the last time this neighborhood had something hot to gossip about?"

"Once we start on Barry Gal, everything else will fall by the wayside," said Elizabeth Donahue.

"I'm with Elizabeth," Eric Hoffman put in. "Barry Gal already won tentative approval from the zoning board to add five thousand square feet to his house. To do that, he'll have to chop down several eucalyptus trees as well as cut off the toe of the hill, which could mean mud slides during the next rainy season."

"You brought him into the neighborhood, Eva," said Elizabeth Donahue. "So tell us what we can do to stop him."

"I didn't invent Barry Gal, I just sold him a house," said Eva Vaine defensively.

"The worst is yet to come," said Marty Gellis. "Barry's going to shoot a new movie that uses our street as its main location. We're going to have production cranes and trucks up the kazoo, and it's a cop movie, so there's going to be lots of guys running up and down the street, shooting at other guys."

"Outrageous," fumed Nancy Mendoza.

"I can't believe he got the necessary permits," said Eva Vaine.

"I'd remind everyone that we're all tied to the movie business in one way or another, so it's a little uncool to protest," said Sidney Garman.

"I don't give a shit," said Tom Patch. "I don't want someone shooting a movie in my front yard. I get enough of that all day."

"This guy's become a nightmare," said Nancy Mendoza. "First the loud parties, the girls coming and going. Now we have him cutting down trees. And shooting a movie."

"If you don't like him, sue him," exhorted Eva Vaine.

"Eva's right," said Eric Hoffman. "We've got to start with the construction plans. That's suit number one."

"He's already got the biggest house on the block," said Nancy Mendoza. "The man lives alone. He doesn't need another five thousand square feet."

"He doesn't live alone," proclaimed Denise Turley as she

swept down the final steps of her circular staircase. "He lives with a painter who is also a sort of caretaker. I should know because I've been fucking him." A mischievous smile lit up her face. "Barry also has a new live-in girlfriend. Maybe he needs the extra space to chase her around."

"Very interesting, Denise," said Tom Patch. "I'll get *Access Hollywood* up here to tape the rest of the meeting."

"Don't get jealous, Tom. You've got enough action of your own," Denise admonished.

"If the association's going to file suit, we need to vote," Todd Plover said. "This action is going to eat into our financial reserves."

"Trouble is, I'll have to abstain," Marty Gellis offered, looking even more pained than usual. "This Gal is paying me ten thousand dollars a month to serve as a consultant to his film company. That's how I know about the cop movie. Mind you, I barely know him, but I don't see how I can vote if I'm cashing his checks."

"At least his checks aren't bouncing," said Sidney Garman.

"One of his movies is on submission to Warner Brothers for distribution," said Eric Hoffman. "Technically I may have to recuse myself as well."

"His tentacles are spreading," Denise Turley said, with a sweeping gesture. "Remember, 'wisdom empowers, but fools with power corrupt.' That's George Bernard Shaw's wisdom, anyway."

"He's just another rich asshole with loads of money," said Elizabeth Donahue.

"I already don't like him," said Denise Turley.

"He obviously thinks he can buy anyone he wants," Todd Plover said.

"We still have enough votes to pass a resolution," Eric Hoffman said. "I'd suggest we do it now before he tosses any more money around."

"So moved," said Elizabeth Donahue.

"Seconded," murmured Marty Gellis. "But I can't vote, of course."

"Can we see a show of hands?" Todd Plover said.

All but two raised their hands. "The motion passes," said Plover.

"So be it," said Hoffman. "I'll get it going tomorrow morning."

"Good," said Garman. "This Gal guy's either going to buy us out or flood us out."

"If there's no other business . . . ," said Plover.

"I think we've exhausted our reservoir of community spirit," Garman said, as everyone started filing out.

The Arbiter

Nancy Mendoza needed air. It had been stuffy in the screening room—and the air conditioning had been balky of late—but Nancy knew that wasn't the problem. The movie had closed in on her—*that* was the problem. She moved quickly down the corridor leading to an open patio. Myra Connolly was keeping pace with her and Nancy tried to ignore her. There was a rule against discussing movies with colleagues immediately after a screening, but Myra tended to ignore it. "That was very intense," Myra said, as Nancy kept walking. "I was really quite moved."

Nancy pushed open the glass door, took out a cigarette and looked back to see Myra's reproachful look. It was perfectly acceptable to light up on the outdoor patio, but Myra, she knew, felt second-hand smoke to be threatening even in an open area. Nancy looked around at the meager plantings, took a deep drag on her cigarette and seated herself on a stone bench. The film, set in Ireland, had gotten under her skin. The basic characters were empathetic—two damaged young people who had come together under appalling circumstances. Both in their late teens, the boy and girl had been seeing each other for a year, but her interest in him had not been reciprocated. They were poor Catholic kids from troubled homes, both of them. Feeling rejected, she had foolishly gone to a club with another boy, a town bully who had raped her, claiming later it was consensual. And then she had done the unthinkable in Ireland: She'd gotten an illegal abortion. Word had seeped out in town and suddenly she was a pariah, except to her original boyfriend who now became her ally, defying social scorn, or perhaps even courting it. After her abortion he'd picked her up in a borrowed car and taken her to an uncle's cabin, brought her food and seen to it she was not bothered. That next night they'd dined together and she was so touched by his loyalty and gentleness that they'd made love.

Well, not exactly. As shot by the young Dublin filmmaker, their scene together was oddly poignant, even innocent. Nancy, however, had fixated on its lurid details, all the while hating herself for doing so. It was a beautiful scene in its own way, but she had developed an early warning system for trouble, and this movie, she sensed, would embroil her in controversy.

What the film showed was simply this: After dinner the two lovers held each other by the fireplace. Because of the abortion, making love was out of the question, but she took out his penis and started petting it as though it were a household pet, and they both smiled sheepishly at this act. Then, off camera, her head disappeared as she took him in her mouth, even as he protested. His penis was shown only fleetingly, and not in a tumescent state, but it was there nonetheless, in defiance of the strictures of the motion picture code that Nancy Mendoza was paid to uphold.

The movie was clearly an art film. Entitled *Bitter Exiles*, it had won awards at two minor festivals prior to its imminent U.S. release. It was the work of a young filmmaker named Sean Solway, who was being heralded as an important artist. Solway already had given contentious interviews with critics on the festival circuit and Nancy intuited that his future fusillades inevitably would be directed at the issue of ratings.

Nancy saw Myra through the glass doors, dabbing at her tears as she chatted with John Holgrove, their portly, pedantic colleague, who was chairman of the twelve-member ratings board. A former teacher and father of four, Holgrove often annoyed Nancy with his lectures on cinema, as though he had access to special insights into filmmaking. But what really irritated her now was something else—her own fixation about the film she'd just seen. Here she'd just spent two hours in intimate proximity with two young lovers, and instead of surrendering to their emotions, she was obsessing about a single image in a single scene. Nothing else in the film was in any way troublesome. There was just the quick shot of the boy's penis followed by the suggestion of fellatio.

This is what her job had done to her, Nancy thought.

Having rated films for three years now, her mind instinctively honed in on potential "problem areas"—the expletives, gestures, sexual contact and acts of violence that could spell controversy. No longer did she see movies, but rather symbols—G, PG-13, R and NC-17. This was the lexicon of the ratings system that she was exceedingly well paid to apply.

Nancy received $100,000 a year with the understanding that she would see between six and eight films a week and help rule over their content. It had been made very clear to her that, though the movie studios effectively paid her salary, she was nonetheless free to exercise her independent judgment. The film industry had established this self-regulatory body to educate parents about the content of movies and also to thwart local censorship groups that had a bad habit of popping up with alarming regularity. Nancy herself had been labeled a "moralistic tyrant" by more than one filmmaker. She had become the bad cop on the ratings board, the toughest negotiator.

Like the other members of the board, Nancy was a parent. While most had three or more kids, Nancy had but one, a precocious fourteen-year-old named Sarah. Her colleagues otherwise represented a sort of Noah's Ark of backgrounds and education levels. There was a carpenter, a hairdresser, a dietitian. Roughly half had gone to college. All looked like poster parents for family values.

Though she hadn't quite measured up in child production, Nancy understood why she'd been selected. Her Hispanic-sounding name was a plus, even though her parents were, in fact, Italian. Her husband, Bernard, despite his name, was a rabbi. Mendoza was an old Portuguese name—his family had been diamond cutters in Lisbon for a span of five generations. Even that counted in her favor. As far as the movie mavens were concerned, her selection took care of two ethnic groups, Hispanics and Jews.

Whatever the politics involved, Nancy had grown intrigued by her curious job. Her salary was more than double what her husband brought home from his rabbinical duties, enabling them to acquire a comfortable three-bedroom home on Starlight Terrace, by far the most modest home on the street. Equally important, her career removed her from the cocoon of housework and the numbing responsibility of ferrying her daughter from lesson to lesson. As far as her husband, Bernard, was concerned, she was not the dedicated homemaker that he had envisioned, but on the other hand he, too, coveted the paycheck.

"Tomorrow morning at ten," John Holgrove was calling out to her, "we must start deliberating over how to deal with this film." Nancy had moved back into the hallway where several of her colleagues had gathered. All were clearly exercised over the movie they had just seen. "We all need to sleep on it," Holgrove added.

Nancy understood his subtext. Holgrove was the most liberal member of the board, usually the first to bend before the passionate arguments of a filmmaker who came begging for a PG-13 rather than an R, or an R rather than an NC-17. Nancy, by contrast, had grown increasingly impatient with the cynical bargaining. If the number of "fuck yous" in a movie were reduced from ten to two, why should that change the rating? she argued. So when Holgrove was advising his colleagues to "sleep on it," Nancy knew he was referring to her.

And as she drove home through the thick afternoon traffic, his implication annoyed her. Coming of age in the turbulent wake of the '70s, she had never thought of herself as conservative. Yet here she sat, in her six-year-old Oldsmobile, swathed in Talbots head to toe—green pleated skirt, button-down blouse, cardigan sweater and loafers. Nancy did not like shopping at Talbots, but Bernard reminded her often to "tone down" her look. She was, after all, a rabbi's wife. The fact that he had married a shiksa already had put a strain on his career, he told her— one that might even bar him from presiding over a prestigious synagogue. Bernard was, to be sure, a Reform rabbi, but in recent years she sensed his yearning for the traditions of the Orthodox. He was a man of ritual who woke up at the same time each day, dressed in the same clothes, ate the same breakfast.

But if Bernard had become an exasperating man, he also remained a very attractive one, with sharp, perfectly etched features and blond, almost albino hair. She had admired him from afar when they were classmates at UCLA, as had her girl friends, and she was astonished when he showed an interest in her. She was more surprised to discover that this blond surfer not only was Jewish but was bent on becoming a rabbi. Nancy had never considered herself a beauty. Dark-haired and a bit pudgy as a teenager, she'd never had money for a proper wardrobe. Her mother, Anna, had worked as a schoolteacher and Nancy's father had long since disappeared into the Los Angeles smog. Anna's message to her two daughters had always been clear: Neither of you are beauties, so work hard, get a good job and don't ever trust a man.

Absorbed in her thoughts, Nancy, by habit, had driven almost to her house before she remembered that other plans had been made for this evening. Sarah, her daughter, was rehearsing for a play and hence had asked for permission to sleep over at a girlfriend's house. Nancy and Bernard had therefore agreed to celebrate their liberation by meeting for dinner. Bernard had picked the place—a somewhat dingy Chinese restaurant on Ventura Boulevard called Won Fu. The room always had a sour smell, Nancy felt, and within hours she was usually suffering that familiar zing associated with MSG, but Bernard loved Chinese food or, more probably, the prices. From college days on, she'd been a cheap date. Indeed, she still picked up the check.

Bernard already was wedged into a table when she arrived. Face buried in the immense menu, he could still pass for a graduate student. At thirty-eight, he had a full head of bushy blond hair and had lately grown a goatee that, to her eye, represented too obvious an attempt to look more maturely rabbinical.

The restaurant already was crowded, and Nancy had to squeeze through the maze of diners to reach him. He gave her a perfunctory kiss as she seated herself.

"There's a new shrimp dish. The couple at the next table tried it," he advised.

"I hate shrimp, as you know," she replied, picking up the menu.

"Order up so we can talk," Bernard instructed, his eyes taking on that semi-squint that she knew portended a contentious discussion. It was the look he assumed when commenting on their daughter's transgressions, which in his mind had become alarmingly frequent. It was also a look assumed during doctrinal soul-searching, when he ruminated aloud whether, for example, they should shift to kosher rules for the household—a precept Nancy flatly rejected.

She and Bernard delivered their orders to a mute Asian who failed to acknowledge their selections in any way, simply scribbling on a pad and vanishing. "I am concerned," Bernard began, tugging several pages from his pocket. "I found these in our home. I do not think it's appropriate material to find in our home. I do not think it is appropriate for you even to possess."

He shoved the pages her way. Glancing at them, she flared. "These are transcripts from an office meeting. Where did you find this?"

"That isn't relevant."

"Relevant, schmelevant. Did you go poking through my desk?"

"It's trash. I am shocked . . ."

Nancy studied the pages now. They were analyses of an action picture that had recently been submitted to the ratings board. Called *Force of Nature*, the movie was violent and steeped in vulgarisms. Nancy had advocated a harsh NC-17 rating and most of her colleagues had agreed, but the studio, eager for a less restrictive R, had offered to eliminate some of the violence and cut back on the four-letter words.

"This is what I do for a living, Bernard," she said. "This is what bought our house."

"The 'f' word—it is mentioned all through that memo." Bernard's pale, almost alabaster, skin reddened as he spoke.

"That's because there were thirty-five instances in which the word 'fuck' was used in this movie. As a result, I took the position that it be rated an adults-only movie."

Bernard's eyes flitted to the tables on each side of theirs. "The word 'cock . . . ' I can't even say it . . ." He spat out the word in a loud whisper.

" 'Cocksucker.' That is the word," she said. "There were twelve times in the movie that this word was used."

"Lower your voice," Bernard demanded. "I am a member of the clergy . . ."

"I am opposed to the use of the word 'cocksucker' at any time in an R movie. Did you read this memo? My position is clear."

"I will not have you using that word. I will not allow memoranda containing that word in our household."

Now it was Nancy whose eyes were narrowing. "Where I work, I am considered a prude, Bernard," she said, enunciating her words carefully. "That's because I take the toughest positions on issues of language and morality. But if I am a prude, then you are a bigot, hiding your head in the sand. You are also a sneak, rifling through my desk like that. What right do you have . . ."

"I was looking for our state tax return," Bernard shot back. "We received a warning today that we are late in filing. I never expected to find . . . trash like this."

"This is not trash. This is a working record of—"

"Obscenities. . . . Rife with obscenities." The two scruffy-looking twenty-somethings seated at the table closest to theirs had now abandoned their own conversation and were carefully monitoring Bernard and Nancy's. One was leaning over so far that the waiter almost knocked him over as he served egg rolls to Nancy and soup to her husband.

"This is my third year on this job," Nancy said, ignoring the food. "You've known all along what my job entails. I've followed your stupid rules—I've never told our friends what I do. Even when they ask us to join them at the movies—movies that I've already seen—I keep my mouth shut. How dare you take this holier-than-thou position!"

"I assumed you were dealing in moral issues."

"We are," she replied. "But this is the real world. We're dealing in moral issues, but we're also bargaining with film-makers about fucks and cocksuckers and motherfuckers and cunts and . . ."

"Stop it!" Bernard shouted. The two kids at the adjacent table were wide-eyed. Bernard's eyes shot from their table to Nancy. He rose, grabbed the pages, then flung them back at her. "I'm out of here," he snapped.

She watched Bernard scurrying toward the exit. She hesitated, then angrily deposited twenty dollars on the table and trailed him out.

The debate about the memorandum was not reprised. Bernard had evening meetings to attend those next few days and arrived home after she was asleep. He seemed distanced each morning at breakfast. On Sunday morning, when they routinely rose early and locked their bedroom door to ensure privacy as they made love, he instead fled the house, citing a morning session he had to attend. Nancy was at once angered and relieved. Their lovemaking, like other aspects of their relationship, had become routinely sedate. Bernard entered her somberly, as though fulfilling some rabbinical obligation. After he came, he promptly washed as though to cleanse himself of sinful behavior.

"Is Daddy worried about something?" her daughter, Sarah, asked absently as Nancy drove her to Hebrew class. "He seems very quiet."

"Perhaps some problem at the synagogue," Nancy replied. "He doesn't confide much." Sarah did not pursue the discussion.

Meanwhile the movie *Bitter Exiles* was generating exactly the controversy that Nancy had feared. The twelve members of the ratings board debated the issue for four hours without resolution. The "liberal" members, led by John Holgrove, argued that it was clearly an art movie, one that would receive a limited release. "The dialogue itself is all but impossible to understand for anyone who has not lived in Ireland," Holgrove pointed out. While an R rating would effectively warn parents of its sexual content and inhibit those under the age of seventeen from attending, the more restrictive NC-17 rating could spell doom for the film. Few newspapers would carry its ads, and only a handful of big-city theaters would even book it.

It fell to Nancy to propound the more restrictive position. "The filmmaker was doubtless sincere," she said, "but there is male frontal nudity in this movie, and we have strictures about that. There must be consistency." Nancy heard her voice shake when she was making her case and it annoyed her. She had become a talented debater during her three years on the board and had long since conquered her nervousness.

"There is no such written restriction," Holgrove countered. "If it's just a question of precedent, I would point out that even the Supreme Court from time to time abandons precedent."

"If we open the door to male frontal nudity, who knows . . ."

"Dammit, Nancy, can't you say the word 'penis'? This 'male frontal' stuff makes you sound like some character out of *The Scarlet Letter.*"

"Have it your way, John," Nancy said. "There is a penis in this movie. There is also a girl who takes that penis into her mouth."

"It happens off camera. You don't see her go down on him," Myra Connolly put in, as usual siding with Holgrove.

"Nancy's position is valid," said John Voland, a rotund man with a woolly beard who was an electrician by trade. A rigid Catholic and a supporter of Pat Buchanan, Voland was Nancy's principal supporter, which always depressed her, but she accepted his vote nonetheless.

"We seem to be deadlocked," Holgrove said. "I propose the following: One of us should meet with the filmmaker . . ."

He consulted his notes. "Sean Solway is his name. There should be a one-on-one. Perhaps he's open to compromise. Nancy might be appeased if the penis was shown in a flash frame . . . something on that order. In fact, Nancy, I would nominate you to take the meeting."

"I second that idea," Voland said, and there were other affirmative nods around the broad conference table.

"I would agree to have a meeting, if that's the consensus," Nancy said. "But don't expect me to succumb to this man's Irish charm, if he has any."

"We are aware of your testosterone level," Myra Connolly said.

"Try to set up the meeting for the next couple of days," Holgrove urged. "The movie is set for release in four weeks."

"What happens if he's still in Ireland?" Nancy asked.

But it turned out Sean Solway had indeed arrived in Los Angeles for meetings with his distributor, Sony Classics. Nancy's assistant reached him at the Chateau Marmont Hotel.

Sean's phone voice was lilting. "Please don't ask me to come to your house of censorship," he pleaded. "I will be hopelessly intimidated. All those people sitting around, snipping scenes. I will be paralyzed for months."

"Sorry. This is where we do our business," Nancy replied crisply.

"So make one exception. I'd even meet you on a street corner. Say Hollywood and Vine."

"My assistant will give you the directions to our office," she said coolly, as she punched "hold."

The next morning at eleven, Nancy found herself confronting a lean, almost skeletal young man with piercing blue eyes, his unruly mane of blond hair splayed haphazardly across the collar of his crumpled work shirt. With his pallor and the dark circles under his eyes, there was something at once callow and fanatical about this young man, Nancy sensed. He eased himself warily into the chair across from Nancy's desk like an animal newly released into a hostile environment.

"So this is where it all happens," Sean said in a virtual whisper. "This is where all the dirty words go to die."

"I never thought of it that way," Nancy said, managing a smile.

"I feel very intimidated," Sean said. "Very naked. I feel like this movie is part of my anatomy and that you will reach out and tear away any portion that you wish."

"Let's not get melodramatic," Nancy said. "We are just an advisory body. And I am one of its functionaries."

Her assistant, Melinda, was at the door. "Can I get you some coffee?" she asked. "Perhaps some water."

"A lager would help," Sean blurted. "Maybe it'll settle me down."

Noticing Melinda's confusion, Nancy said, "I'm afraid we don't have beer. Would you settle for a Pellegrino?"

But Sean didn't seem to hear. "This building—it feels very antiseptic. Does someone go through each night to sterilize the place?"

"We don't go quite that far."

"And the children? I was surprised to see a group of children clambering down the hall as I came in. Do they help snip out the dirty words?"

Nancy shook her head. "This is what we call 'family day,' " she explained. "The organization believes our kids should have some sense of where their parents work, so once a year they visit in the morning, see the offices, the screening rooms."

"And they see you snipping?"

"We don't 'snip,' Mr. Solway. And they don't see the films that we see. We show them some animated films. Family stuff."

"Nothing to pollute their dear little minds."

"Exactly," Nancy said. "But the word 'pollute' was your choice, not mine."

"But you feel my movie has the potential to pollute?"

"You get down to business quickly, don't you?"

"You didn't ask me here to tour with the children. You invited me here to snip. To sanitize."

"Then I take it you read our recommendations. You made a very moving film, Mr. Solway . . ."

"Please stop with the Mr. Solway stuff . . ."

" . . . and we have problems with only one scene."

"This is a very personal film, please understand. This is the story of my younger sister. She and her boyfriend . . . they are the bitter exiles. My country has blotted them out. Like insects."

"And I don't want to detract from the power of your story . . ."

"They are afraid to release *Bitter Exiles* in Ireland. Even in Britain they await the American opening. If it does business here, if it finds acceptance, then we have a chance for a wide opening back home. We have a chance to move people and to affect people's lives."

Nancy took a breath. She shuffled through some papers on her desk. Sean Solway was an intense young man. She felt as though the temperature of the room were rising rapidly.

"So fix that one scene. Just do the 'snip,' as you put it. That will solve the problem."

Sean turned away, his arms flailing. "What is it that so offends you? We are not dealing with some vile, unnatural act. We are displaying this boy's pathetic little willy. A soft blob of flesh. Why does that bother you?"

"It's full frontal nudity. It's against the rules."

"Does that scene move you?"

"That's not the criterion."

"Do any films move you?"

Nancy turned away. She pressed the intercom. "Would you get us two Pellegrinos, Melinda?" She turned back to face Sean Solway.

"Sean, let me confide something. At this point in the discussion I would normally make a little speech, informing you that I am not trying to dictate how you edit your movie, that you are free to release your film with an NC-17 rating or with no rating at all. That is the pat speech, okay?"

"Okay. I get it. But . . . ?"

"But I have learned the details of your deal with Sony

Classics. I know you are required to deliver a film with an R rating. That's your deal. So I am telling you what you must do to get the R."

"And how is it that you happen to know my contract? Do you have spies at the distributors?"

"We have friends. We check around. What difference does it make?"

"It makes a big difference. It takes away my bargaining position. It's a violation of my privacy."

"Sean, we're talking about maybe ten seconds of material here . . ."

"We're talking about cutting a scene that most people find very moving. A scene that means a great deal to me."

"It's not my intention to hurt your film, Sean. I don't think—"

But Sean Solway was on his feet, looming over her now. "You are a very complex woman, Mrs. Mendoza," he intoned. "Your words signal danger, but your eyes signal empathy."

Nancy met his gaze. She flushed. "I am not important," she said. "We are talking rules."

"Your rules."

"We all need rules."

"It's truth that is in short supply, not rules." And Sean Solway turned and left her office.

Nancy did not tell Bernard of the meeting. As she put down their meat loaf dinner, Bernard was reading and making notes and Sarah was asking questions about her homework.

The following morning an e-mail from John Holgrove

awaited her at her office. "Let's talk," was all it said. A conversation with Holgrove, she knew, usually entailed a walk down the street to Starbucks. Holgrove liked to talk and didn't like to listen. She checked her watch. In forty-five minutes there would be another screening. That was good news—Holgrove could prattle on only till then.

They found a corner table at Starbucks. Adjacent to them was a young man bent over his laptop. He wore a headset and was fielding phone calls as he worked and sipped coffee.

"You have eight votes," Holgrove told her somberly. "I have only four. *Bitter Exiles* will get an NC-17, which is a terrible injustice. Unless, that is, you can persuade him to take out that scene."

"He won't budge. You know the type—they never budge."

"No one will see his film. It's a pity. There are not enough good movies out there and we shouldn't be blocking . . ."

"I, too, have lost tough votes this year, John," Nancy replied. "I lost on that disgusting movie *South Park*, which should have gone out with an NC-17. Even the subtitle was vile—*Bigger, Longer and Uncut*."

"We reviewed it six times. We removed the most offensive material."

"I don't think so. *Boogie Nights*—another R movie that should have gotten an NC-17. And that Kubrick movie, *Eyes Wide Shut*, naked women all over the place and we gave that an R."

"We made them take out the humping . . ."

"What difference did that make? The men and women

were obviously fornicating. And with an R, you know as well as I do that children will be able to sneak into those theaters in the multiplex."

Holgrove took a long sip on his coffee. "Nancy, I know you're married to a member of the clergy. I realize you're a religious woman and all . . ."

"I'm not, you know. Not religious, that is. Not really. I mean, I was raised a Catholic . . ."

"A Catholic. But you're married to a rabbi . . ."

"None of that matters, John. You want to give me another one of your lectures about being too rigid. You're going to tell me that society has grown more permissive and so should our movies."

"All I want you to think about is this: The movies out there are shit. The few movies we see that reflect true artistic merit—inevitably they push the envelope. They tend to be sexy, even violent. We cannot discourage those movies, Nancy. We cannot crush the few voices that have something to tell us."

"You're telling me I'm a prig. Okay, I hear you. Message received. Now let's get back to our office. We have another movie to see and, from what I hear, it, too, will be pure shit."

The movie that awaited them that afternoon was worse than even she expected. It was a private eye movie set in Los Angeles, circa 1945—a lame imitation of *L.A. Confidential.* The direction was appalling. And there were two scenes that seemed to have been inserted only to give the filmmaker bargaining position. In one a woman was tied to a bed and repeatedly violated by two men. There was also a thoroughly gross torture scene, in which a red-hot iron was slammed against the naked buttocks of a woman hostage. Nancy knew the tactic all too well: These scenes would be taken out if other problem areas were overlooked. The cynical negotiating ploys left her weary.

Melinda, Nancy's assistant, intercepted her as she returned to her office. "Sarah called on her cell," she said. "She wanted to remind you she needs a ride to karate class."

"I'd forgotten . . ."

"Kids take a lot of classes, don't they?" Melinda said. "In my day, we never had all these classes."

"My daughter has taken everything from tap dancing to digital filmmaking. My husband says I encourage her, but it's the opposite."

That afternoon Sarah seemed preoccupied as they wound along Laurel Canyon, heading for Ventura Boulevard in the Valley. "Anything you want to talk about?" Nancy said finally.

"Do you want to talk about that movie?" Sarah said timorously.

"What movie is that?"

"The movie Mr. Holgrove showed me. *Bitter Exiles*."

Nancy had to swerve to miss the curb on her next turn. "Be careful, Mom," Sarah said nervously.

"Will you run that by me one more time, Sarah? Did you say *Bitter Exiles*?"

"Yeah. The Irish picture."

"When did you see it?"

"Yesterday. When we visited the offices. He showed the

other kids the usual Disney stuff. But he asked me to see this Irish movie. Alone."

"That son of a bitch."

"Who? Mr. Holgrove? He's a really nice man."

"But he had no right . . ."

"It's an awesome movie, Mom. I cried."

Nancy almost missed another curve. "Please slow down, Mom."

"Did he give any reason for showing it to you?"

"He said you and he were talking about it a lot. That it was an example of the sort of work you do together."

"It's not a movie for children . . ."

"And I am not 'children,' in case you forgot. I'm fourteen, for God's sake.'

"That movie is restricted. It won't even qualify for an R rating."

"Why? I mean, those kids. The way their families turned on them. When her boyfriend decided to stick by her . . . that put me away. It was awesome."

"But there was material in the film that's simply inappropriate . . ."

"What are you talking about?"

"Mr. Holgrove and I have to give movies a rating, Sarah. That's our job. That's what I'm talking about."

"So what's wrong with this movie?"

Nancy took a breath. "The . . . fellatio scene."

"Oh, for God's sake, Mother. There's nothing shocking about . . ."

"She took his penis . . ."

"I barely remember that scene. Who gives a shit?"

"Sarah, she took his penis and . . ."

"Mom, every girl in school who wants to keep her boyfriend—"

"Shut up, Sarah."

"There's even a girl who gives lessons. She's a senior and she teaches the younger girls how to do it. It's cool . . ."

"That's the most disgusting thing . . ."

"You're living in the last century and you're supposed to be rating pictures? I don't get it. You're as fuzzy-brained as Dad."

"Let's change the subject."

"It was an awesome movie, Mom."

"He had no right to show it to you."

"Sure. I'm better off watching *Sex and the* fucking *City*?"

"Don't be foul-mouthed, Sarah. If your father ever heard you . . ."

"My father never listens to me, so how could he hear me?"

The next morning Nancy marched to Holgrove's office before she even dropped off her briefcase or checked her calls. Holgrove got to his feet the moment he saw her.

"All right, I know I'm in for it."

"How could you? There's such a thing as parental consent."

"Okay, I owe you an apology. It was impulsive of me."

"Impulsive? It was just plain stupid."

"I saw Sarah walking down the hallway apart from the other kids. And it suddenly occurred to me . . . what would she think? She's fourteen and all. How would this strike her?"

"Are you out of your mind? Would you want me to run *South Park* for your kids?"

"Look, I apologize. You could get me canned for this. I know that."

"I'm really disappointed in you, John." She was walking briskly to her office when she heard John Holgrove trudging after her.

"Nancy . . . ?"

She turned.

"It was a shitty thing to do. Not asking you first . . ."

"She loved the movie, John. She said it was 'awesome.' She cried."

A wan smile creased Holgrove's face. "And the scene?"

"It was like she didn't even notice. I had to ask her."

"Kids. You never know. They inhabit a different world."

"I really hate what I do, John. I mean, we're supposed to set the rules, but whose rules?"

"It's a living."

Nancy attended another screening that morning. It was a sappy comedy modeled after *American Pie*. Nancy took down fourteen passages that required editing. Her assistant flagged her as she was returning to her office.

"That Irish director . . . he wants to 'buy you a pint.' That was his message."

Nancy shook her head. "That's cute. He wants to buy me off with a drink."

"He suggested tomorrow. The bar at the Bel-Air Hotel.

He said that would be 'uppity' enough for you. His word—uppity. I told him no."

"Tell him yes," Nancy said quickly.

"But you never . . ."

"I could use 'a pint,' " she said.

The snug paneled bar at the Bel-Air was relatively empty the next evening when Nancy walked in. Two silver-haired CEO types were talking over scotch at one corner table. Across the room an elderly couple sipped on their drinks, looking bored. Sean Solway was sitting alone at the bar. Nancy thought he looked hilariously out of place.

As she joined him, she was startled when he gave her a quick peck on each cheek. His clothes smelled mildewed, as though they'd weathered too much Irish mist.

"Thanks for coming," he said. "I was sure you'd never leave your lair at snip city."

"I'm here," Nancy said.

"So I heard what happened this morning. I heard and I wanted to thank you."

"News travels fast."

"I was right about your eyes. Kind eyes, taut lips."

The bartender was standing before them. "Can I get you folks anything?"

"Just water," Nancy said. "No, make that a vodka martini. Straight up."

Sean smiled. "A lager, please," he said. Then he signaled the bartender. "No, make that the same as the lady."

"Look, Sean, this business about the rating—the only

thing anyone can know is that the board voted to give your film an R rating, rather than an NC-17. Without condition."

"But I know you had to change your vote to make that happen."

"And you also know I can't comment on that."

"But I can thank you, can't I? I can thank you for understanding my movie."

Their drinks arrived. Sean raised his glass. They clinked. He smiled. "I would never ask you what made you change your vote. I'd never ask you that."

"And I would never answer."

"Exactly."

She stared at her glass. "Have you ever had the feeling that you've become someone who is in fact a stranger to you?"

"I was working for an ad agency in Dublin three years ago. I suddenly heard myself pitching a client one day and I said to myself, 'Who in God's name is that pitchman?' And I quit the next day to make my film."

Nancy smiled. "I can't quit. Not until my daughter gets through college. It's a job, you know."

"Well, what the hell. They pay you to watch movies . . ."

". . . terrible movies . . ."

". . . and to do your snipping . . ."

"I hope your movie does well, Sean. I mean that."

"In the end, it's just a movie."

When they left the bar, he kissed her again. And this time she kissed him back.

Second Coming

There are survival rules for every profession, and as a twenty-year career flack, I've worked out mine. For example: Never take a long plane ride with a client. When you're the press agent for a movie star, one thing you don't want to do is sit next to him for eight hours. You don't want to hear him kvetch. You don't want to know about his love life. In fact, you really don't want to know much about him at all for one important reason: There's nothing worth knowing.

All of which explains why I was thoroughly pissed to find myself next to Tom Patch on Delta Flight 1288 from Nice to New York. Sure, I'd been his press agent for twelve years and he'd become a major star, but even as we buckled up I knew I didn't want to be there. Not for an eight-hour flight. Not for a one-hour flight. Our personal contact had always been limited to half-hour bursts when there was usually an interview taking place, or maybe we were at a premiere. But eight hours! How could this happen!

I knew how it could happen. Tom had been invited to the Cannes Film Festival for the premiere screening of his latest film, a re-make of the old radio show *Gangbusters*. Warner Brothers had flown him over on its corporate jet and was also set to fly him back to L.A., but the plane developed engine trouble in London and the studio said its back-up jet was flying Bruce Willis on a junket to Berlin, and suddenly the only option left was to fly commercial. Tom received this news like any movie star would—he had a shit fit. He locked himself in his suite at the Hotel du Cap and said he wouldn't come out "until the fucking studio lived up to its fucking commitments." All of which translated into a mandate to me. Suddenly I was responsible, not the studio. I reminded him that he had committed to do the *Today* show in New York the next morning and that hiding out at the Hotel du Cap was not an option. Mind you, I had to tell him this on the phone since he wouldn't let anyone into his suite except room service. The reason was that he'd picked up a hot young French photojournalist the night before to reinforce his reputation as one of the screen's great lovers.

Anyway, I booked us on a nonstop Delta flight to New York and discovered that the only open seats were next to each other. Tom had another shit fit when he realized Delta had no first class—just an extended business class. "I don't ride business class," he hissed. "I thought your job was to protect me from these surprises." I felt like replying that, no, my job was only to get your face on the *Today* show and to prevent your fans from finding out that you were a narcissistic asshole who would fuck a snail, but I decided that this was not the moment for an ego confrontation. In fact, there'd never be such a moment.

And Tom Patch wasn't worse than any of the rest of them. There was a decent side to him, in fact, a basic loyalty and even a glimmer of intelligence. Unlike most actors who'd broken through, he still retained the same agent, manager and press agent. Despite his temper tantrums, directors liked working with him. He still called his mother once a week, or at least took her calls. She was a pleasant Czech lady named Tania who'd been widowed when her Irish cop husband died of a heart attack, and Tom had grown up poor in Tenafly, New Jersey, though the official studio bio said his father died heroically in a police shoot-out. I'd met Tom when he was a struggling kid actor Off-Broadway, and I'd known right away he was a comer. He was a great-looking kid whose working-class macho was softened by a sort of Montgomery Clift–like vulnerability that he could turn on and off at will. In truth, Tom Patch was about as vulnerable as a fire hydrant, which was just as well, given the chain of rejection every kid actor has to endure. But the parts soon started coming, then TV gigs and suddenly he was earning $11 million a movie plus a piece of the back end and studios were lined up to catch his next available "slot."

Did all this success fuck with his head? Does the sun set in the west? I've been running my PR firm, Stanley Harmon Associates, since the early '80s, and I've never represented a star who wasn't a narcissistic dick head. How can it be otherwise? I mean, they walk into a room and attention is riveted on them. Everyone strains to hear their every chance remark or cater to their every whim. Every girl wants to fuck 'em. Every producer wants to slip them a script. Every agent wants to sign them. Every reporter wants an interview. Every maitre d' wants to lead them to the best table and usually doesn't even give them the bill. And even if their last movie sucked, some studio will still raise their payday next time out.

Tom's deal on *Gangbusters* was a case in point. Not only did he get $11 million against 7½ percent of the gross receipts, but the studio also threw in a chef, a personal trainer, a double, a personal makeup man, an assistant and the use of a private jet during principal photography. And just to keep him happy, the studio also donated hotel suites and first-class airline tickets to location for any of Tom's friends who wanted to drop by.

Only now there was no private jet and Tom and I were side by side at 35,000 feet and a flight attendant was hovering over us. "Can I get you a drink?" she asked with that pleasant plastered-on stew smile. "I'd like a mimosa," I said. Tom kept staring out the window. "The same," he mumbled.

The stew didn't hear him. "Could you repeat that?"

Tom turned toward her. "Mimosa."

"I really liked your last film," said the stew, not missing a beat. She was tall and willowy but thoroughly businesslike, and she obviously understood actors, because she didn't wait around for an acknowledgment. "What's her problem?" Tom said to me.

"You have eight hours to find out," I told him.

Tom adjusted his watch to New York time. "Christ, we're

gonna get to the hotel at midnight and I'm supposed to be bushy-tailed at dawn."

"The limo is picking you up at six A.M. I know you prefer Katie Couric over Matt, so I got a commitment for her to interview you. That wasn't easy, so show some appreciation."

Tom feigned a few claps of his hands. "Are they showing a clip?"

"I sent them the scene with you picking up Meg Ryan in the club. I figured we'd show you doing what you do best."

"Meg wasn't too good in that scene," Tom said.

"Hey, you got the close-up, not her."

The stew set mimosas in front of each of us.

"Were you two at the festival?" she said.

"Yeah," said Tom. "It was a zoo."

"I always wanted to visit that zoo," she offered, moving off.

"Nice ass," Tom said as she left. "I like her look."

"Ever see a stew you didn't like?"

"Hey, most of them are old enough to be my ma," he said.

"Maybe an older woman would be good for you. Settle you down."

I felt Tom's gaze. "Why are you on my case today?"

"Is this my cue to get on my knees and beg forgiveness?"

"I mean, I'm in a tense mode. I'm flying commercial. And tomorrow is staring me in the face."

"Come on, you've done the *Today* show maybe twenty times . . ."

"It's not about TV. It's about the big Four-Oh. It's about my fuckin' birthday."

I had always been good about getting clients' special days onto my computer. I knew Tom's was approaching and I'd even told my office to buy him a gift—one of those $5,000 leather chairs that reclines and gives you a massage. But the "40" milestone had escaped my attention. I'd been routinely subtracting three years from his official bio—per his mandate—to the point where even I had lost track. But Tom hadn't, and he was clearly bent out of shape.

"I hadn't forgotten," I lied. "I just didn't want to rub it in . . ."

"I'm depressed, man," Tom said. "I mean . . . forty. That's middle age. That's adulthood. That's beyond adulthood—it's decrepitude."

"Have another swig of that mimosa, kid . . ."

"Do I look forty? You can level with me. You're my press agent, for Chrissake."

"What do you want me to say? That you look twenty? You don't look twenty. You look maybe thirty-two. That's a good look for you, Tom. You're not the kid lover anymore, you're the mature leading man. Those roles command bigger paychecks . . ."

"Fuck 'mature.' I'm not ready for 'mature.' "

"Are you ready for some nuts? Or crackers?" The tall stew was hovering again. She had big brown eyes and there was an openness to her face. Tom reacted to her.

"You from New York?"

"Now I am. I was born in Raleigh. Another one of those southern girls who liked the big city. My name is Nola, in case you need anything." And she was off again.

I finished my mimosa. "You see, that girl looks thirty-two," I said. "She looks mature, but she also looks sexy."

"She looks hot."

"So there's nothing wrong with 'mature,' got it?"

Tom wrestled a script out of his leather carry-on and shuffled its pages for a couple of minutes, but he was clearly distracted.

"Look, 'mature' doesn't work for me. Not yet, anyway. You know why? 'Cause ever since high school I've let my dick lead me around. I am my dick. That's my identity."

"What's with this sudden burst of introspection, Tom? It doesn't become you."

"It's 'cause suddenly I'm forty. I mean, I know you think I'm a shallow piece of shit, but I'm . . ."

"Cut it out, kid. I've always known you've got the smarts. Otherwise, you wouldn't have gotten to where you are."

"Don't start sucking up . . ."

"Okay, so you don't want to be forty. It's not such a bad age. It's not like you're sixty . . ."

"Hey, I'm an actor, remember? Millions of people stare at my face. That's like my brand—my goddamn face!"

"So that's the good news. You still got a great young face."

"That's been my problem, Stanley. When I was fifteen years old I stared in the mirror one morning and I said to myself, 'Holy shit, that's me.' "

"Hey, all of us look in the mirror when we're fifteen. That goes with the territory. The difference is that when actors stare in the mirror they love what they see. The rest of us hate what we see."

Tom nodded ruefully. "Yeah, I remember thinking, 'I like what I see.' And the girls were all calling suddenly and even my older sister kept telling me I was hot. She even got me into a school play."

"And you decided you'd be a movie star. That's how it happens. Don't complain about it. It's a great life."

"So who's complaining?" Tom tossed his unread script under his seat. "I need another drink. Where's that 'mature' stew?"

I signaled for the flight attendant. She didn't see me, so I pushed the call button, which she didn't answer. Tom shot me a look. Clearly he hadn't yet given up on his introspective episode.

"The trouble with you, Stanley, is that you still think I don't know I'm an asshole."

"Come off it, kid."

"I love myself. I admit it. My world revolves around me. I admit that. I like it that way."

"So you should be at peace with the world."

"Except I know it's not enough. I need more."

"More of what?"

"That's the trouble. I don't know. Just more."

"I can tell you what you're going to get more of. More money. More fame. More women."

"But none of that is really 'more.' "

"Does that mean you want more mimosa?" Nola, the stew, was smiling. She had picked up the tail end of our conversation and was clearly amused. Tom saw that, too.

"See what I'm up against?" he said. "I just told my associ-

114

ate here that I need something more in life, and he doesn't get it."

"Not everyone can get profound at thirty-five thousand feet," she said with a twinkle. "Trust me. I spend most of my life at high altitudes."

Nola and Tom exchanged a quick smile. If they were going to hook up, the best thing for me to do was to stay out of the way.

"I'll bring you your drinks. Also the dinner menu," Nola said. "And I should warn you that the lady in seat 8B would like your autograph. So would two people in coach, one of whom is a grandma who would like me to take a photo of you with her."

"Thanks for the warning," Tom said.

Nola darted off on her appointed mission. "I like her," Tom said. "She's one of those women who's always one step ahead of you."

"One of those 'mature' women," I said. "Look, I don't want to break your train of thought, but I heard you promise the William Morris agent you'd have that script read by the time we land."

Tom picked up the script from under the seat. "It's another cop picture," he said. "I can tell from page one that I've read this script before, that I've played this character before."

"There's probably a fifteen-million-dollar firm offer on the table, so try to get to page twenty before the third mimosa hits you," I said. "Then I'll give you a sleeping pill."

Nola delivered the drinks along with some scraps of paper

for Tom's autograph, but she didn't stick around to chat. Thankfully, Tom became immersed in his script, which gave me a chance to deal with my e-mail and catch up on *Vanity Fair, Time, Newsweek* and *GQ*. Dinner arrived in the form of reconstituted chicken breast and mushy rice that tasted like it had been pre-chewed. After dinner I took a Sonata, which always guaranteed four hours of sleep. I also gave one to Tom, but he set his aside.

The next thing I knew, someone had stepped on my foot and I was suddenly awake. "Sorry," Tom said as he fell back into his seat.

"What time is it?"

"You've been dead to the world for four hours."

"And you?"

"I've been talking with Nola."

I should have known. At the start of the flight he'd been complaining that he wouldn't have enough time to sleep, but that wouldn't deter him from picking up one more stew. He was pathological. He was an actor!

"I'm sure you made her day," I offered.

"She's cool," he said. "Sexy and cool."

"And you'll have four hours of sleep max tonight."

"I don't need much sleep. Besides, I don't like to sleep alone."

"Feel free not to share that information with Katie Couric tomorrow morning."

"Look, nothing's going to happen. I mean, this one . . . Nola . . . she's different."

"Why different?"

"Just different."

"So is she going home with you or not?"

"Why do you have to know?"

"'Cause I ordered one limo to take us to the St. Regis. If you're taking her with you, we need two limos."

Tom shot me a look. "I'll keep you posted."

At that point I apparently dozed off again, only to awaken to a stew's voice advising that we would shortly be on approach to Kennedy. Tom's seat was empty. I realized I had to pee desperately so I made my way to the front of the plane. Two other passengers had gotten the same idea since the "occupied" light was on for both toilets. As I waited, I heard a familiar voice. Tom was talking to the stew in the galley. Realizing he couldn't see me, I started to step forward to say something, but froze when I heard their words.

"We'll be on approach any moment," Nola was saying. "That means you must take your seat and I must go about my routine. I've enjoyed our chat."

"Don't give me this 'enjoyed our chat' shit," Tom said. "I need an answer."

"I've given you the answer."

"Why are you doing this?"

"Look, I don't want to hurt your feelings . . ."

"Hey, I'm an actor. I have no feelings."

"You really don't have a clue, do you?"

"Clue? What clue?"

"Because we had this same conversation maybe fourteen

months ago. Maybe sixteen. The same conversation. You were adorable then, too."

"What . . . what are you telling me?" Tom sounded devastated. I'd never heard that voice before.

"Tom, baby, you're losing it. You came on to me on an L.A. to New York flight. You came on strong and I said yes and we went to your hotel and spent the night."

"You're putting me on, aren't you?"

The door to one of the toilets popped open and a passenger got out. I started to enter, but I couldn't leave the conversation at this point. I moved into the toilet but left the door open a crack.

"Your pitch was wonderful last year, too, but when we got to your hotel, well, let's just say you were tired. Real tired. You actually were so tired you nodded off over dinner," Nola said. "When we got to your suite you were very nice, but you fell asleep in the middle. It was really sort of boring."

"Oh, fuck," Tom said.

"Well, we did fuck, but you had to rush off to do one of those morning TV interview shows and, well, as I said, you were very nice and all. And you don't remember. That figures."

"Well . . ."

"See, that's the trouble. You were my big movie star date and I was just another stew. I even remember that you had a big freckle on your penis. I'd never seen a freckled penis before." Then I heard Tom chuckle, then she laughed, too. And I saw them sort of embrace just as I shut the door.

By the time I returned to my seat, Tom was buckled up and the plane was starting to hit bumps as we neared the runway. Tom was quiet.

"You okay?" I asked.

"I've just had a daunting experience," he said in a whisper.

"Why daunting?" Of course, I couldn't tell him I'd overheard it.

"Let's just say it confirmed my worst suspicions. I mean, it's all coming together. I'm turning forty. It's time to change things, is all."

"It's just a birthday, Tom. Just another number."

"It's time to change," he mumbled again.

Later, we took two limos to the hotel. Tom and Nola shared the first one, and I took the second. They seemed very comfortable together. More than comfortable. They seemed downright cozy.

Tom did great with Katie Couric the next morning. He didn't look tired at all. If anything, he seemed to have a glow about him.

I went home to L.A. and a week later he was on the phone. He was still at the St. Regis! He was talking real fast; too fast for me to follow. ". . . don't want any press to know. You can tell them the morning after. No photo ops, nothing. I want it to be quiet. 'Dignified,' is the way Nola put it . . ."

"Okay, slow down, Tom. You lost me somewhere. What's this about?"

"The wedding."

"Okay. Got it. Whose wedding?"

"Me and Nola. Tomorrow morning, eleven o'clock. St. Marks Episcopal Church in the Village. That's her church."

"Her church . . ."

"You're invited, of course. There will be just eleven of us. Maybe twelve . . ."

"You and Nola. You don't mind if I sound surprised?"

"Why surprised? Remember when I said I wanted more?"

"Sure, but . . ."

"Well, Nola is more. Meeting her again, I realized . . . well . . . I'd been around the course. I'd been around without learning much. It was time to stop."

"But, marriage . . . This isn't like spin the bottle. I mean, the bottle pointed to her, but—"

"I love her, Stanley. And you're invited."

"I'll be there."

"And no press. Dignified wedding."

"Hey, you caught me by surprise, kid. Congratulations. I'm proud of you."

"You once told me that none of your clients ever change. You still believe that?"

"Not anymore."

He hung up. I found myself staring at the receiver for a beat. Okay, Tom Patch hit forty and he grew up.

Or something.

Friend of the Family

Shoving open the door of the Warner Brothers commissary, Eric Hoffman felt dyspeptic. His lunch had consisted of a steak, as mandated by his Atkins diet, but he could visualize the lump of meat squatting contemptuously in his stomach. Part of the problem he felt could be traced not to the food but to his luncheon companion. Helen Meigher, the studio's chief of Human Resources, reminded him of his school principal, always alert to infractions of the rules, real or imagined. Slender and vulpine, Miss Meigher was insistent about reviewing a spate of sexual harassment suits, most of them involving gay employees, and her approach to the issue struck Eric as needlessly clinical, monetizing every furtive encounter in the men's room, every chance groping in the gym, all the while computing the payment required to minimize the studio's legal risk.

But if the lunch had left him vaguely depressed, the agenda for his next meeting seemed even more oppressive. True,

Eric's life was one of relentless negotiation, hammering away at the demands of agents and attorneys representing stars and star directors. His adversaries were the best hagglers in the business—skilled advocates who fancied themselves as white-collar warriors. But the meeting that now confronted him entailed more than mere negotiation. It was about a personal war—one that the studio assumed Eric would resolve through forceful intervention.

Yet making peace was not Eric's specialty, as he had pointed out to Derek Kirsh, the studio's president of production, a glib, young Harvard M.B.A. who was, at best, a selective listener. "This feud has to end," Kirsh had instructed Eric at a midmorning staff meeting. "It's gotten into the trades. It's going to hurt the movie. You can't have a producer and director mouthing off against each other without hurting the movie." A bulky man who was all smooth surfaces and looked younger than his forty-five years, Kirsh had made a clumsy effort to resolve the fight, but had failed. It had now fallen to Eric to step into the breach, partly because he had a history with Bert Karlin, the producer, who was regarded as the principal troublemaker. When Eric was a young lawyer in private practice, Karlin was one of his clients and they had maintained a loose friendship, playing golf together a few times a year. But Eric knew Karlin to be a caustic, egotistical man who liked to nurture his feuds. Settling Karlin's dispute with Jake Weberman, his director, would be far from easy. "It's way beyond the point where you sit down over a drink and get these guys to hug each other. Besides, their egos thrive on war. They're fueled by it," Eric had said.

To be sure, Eric had come up with a tactic, one that carried great risk. He had started to explain that strategy to Kirsh, but his attention span had clicked off. The message was clear: It was up to Eric Hoffman, the studio consigliere, to resolve this mess. The top guys didn't want to know the hows or whys.

That's what riled Eric as he walked back to his office, moving past rows of squat stucco structures. Why was it left to him to deal with these two uniquely unpleasant sociopaths? He was a dealmaker, not a peacemaker. The production guys liked to take the credit for the successes, but whenever trouble loomed, they were nowhere to be found.

Suddenly Eric was sneezing. Someone was cutting the lawn and his allergies were erupting accordingly. The patches of lawn had always struck Eric as some sort of bucolic affectation. Maybe Jack Warner and his kin in the old days had liked this faux college campus look, but Eric had never understood it. There wasn't any grass on the classic old lots in Hollywood. None on the old MGM lot, either, which now was owned by Sony. Why did Warners still need grass? he thought, sneezing again.

Exacerbating Eric's distress was the fact that he had seen this problem coming. He had cobbled together the deal on *Crossroads*, had secured the rights to the novel just before it hit the best-seller lists, had negotiated contracts for Jake Weberman to direct and Bert Karlin to produce. He had never quite understood the logic to the project, however. Weberman's last two films were moneymakers, but they were violent cop films. Weberman was a tough-talking filmmaker, a man known for his swagger—not the obvious candidate to handle a sensitive teenage love story like *Crossroads*. Karlin's last two credits consisted of a sci-fi project and a World War II film, but he, too, had a passion for *Crossroads*, sensing perhaps that it would score with the vast youth audience out there.

Eric felt another stomach pang as he shoved open the door to the two-story building that housed his office. With its white stucco facade and its green shutters, the building had a deceivingly benign look, but within its walls feral M.B.A.s were hammering out deals even as development troops were carving up scripts. This was not a quiet, collegial place. It was a place for crunchers, like Eric, and if he had his way he would erect the sort of severe black high-rises that dominated the Universal Pictures lot on the other side of the hill.

Eric checked his watch. It was 2:27. Climbing the steps, he hoped that his combatants had not yet arrived. Sitting in his waiting room, however, sat a pale, stoic man in a gray suit looking, Eric thought, like an insurance actuary. Paul Wilkie had remained exactly as he'd remembered him.

They shook hands. Wilkie's were oddly smooth, his handshake limply noncommittal, and Eric wondered how a man like this could end up occupying such a curious corner of the legal business.

"Good to see you again," Eric lied. Surely Wilkie knew Eric had hoped never to see him again. That was the way it was in Wilkie's line of work.

"Thank you for setting up this meeting," Wilkie said.

"These two men, Karlin and Weberman, my office was having trouble locating them. We were getting concerned. But I remembered your studio affiliation."

"Look, this meeting could get a little emotional," Eric warned. "These two—they don't get along. They're doing a movie together, but it's not going smoothly."

"I do not relate to the movie business," Wilkie said.

"That's okay. Not many people do. We'll get through it."

Wilkie followed him into his office, a spacious if cluttered room, dominated by a large green sofa, three bulky white easy chairs and a glass coffee table. To one side was Eric's desk, on which were strewn an array of deal memos and legal briefs. Interspersed among them were clusters of yellow Post-it notes, reflecting Eric's frenzied battle to keep pace with calls to be returned and negotiations to pursue.

Wilkie was about to seat himself even as Bert Karlin's wide frame filled the doorway. A thick man with unruly red hair, a knob of a nose and a jutting chin, Karlin suggested aggression in his very posture. He seemed to be in motion even when standing still. He started to say something to Eric but stopped in midsentence, startled by Wilkie's presence.

"Wilkie, isn't it? What're you doing here?" Karlin asked in a throaty bark.

"Technical assistance," Eric put in.

"A face from the past," Karlin said. "What's it been—fourteen years?"

"It's been fifteen, actually," Wilkie said.

"This isn't about Molly, is it? She's a good girl, doing just fine. Her birth mother isn't wanting her back, is she? We've had your assurances . . ."

"Nothing of that sort," Wilkie said.

Karlin's face was flushed. "It would kill Doris if she ever lost that kid."

"Relax, Bert," Eric said. "Wilkie's not on that sort of mission."

"Then what the hell . . . ? I mean, it sort of shakes you up when the lawyer you hired to adopt your kid suddenly materializes fifteen years later."

The intercom sounded. Eric glanced at his screen, then said to his secretary, "Show him in." Eric watched Karlin react as Jake Weberman warily entered his office. Tall and gangly, with thinning black hair and a manic gaze, Weberman did not seem at first like the hell-raiser Eric knew him to be.

Now it was Weberman who was sizing up the room. "What sort of meeting is this?" he said. "I see my life passing before me—my estranged producer, the lawyer who brought me my beloved son, that is you, isn't it, Wilkie?"

Wilkie nodded stiffly as Weberman continued his rant. "So in the middle here we find the studio consigliere and I wonder, what have these three men got to do with one another? Like, what is the subtext here?"

"Skip the elaborate scenarios, Jake," Eric put in. "This meeting is simply about facing up to one's responsibilities."

"For this we need Paul Wilkie?" said Karlin. "I thought he was in the baby business, not the movie business."

Eric took a deep breath. Here's where he was entering uncharted waters.

"This is weird stuff," Weberman said. "I don't like weird."

"Nothing weird about it," Eric said. "You and I and Karlin have one important thing in common. We all adopted babies with the help of Mr. Wilkie here. Since he was unable to find you, Wilkie contacted me through the studio and asked me to set up a meeting. That is what I have done."

"So we're meeting. What are we meeting about?" demanded Karlin.

All eyes were on Wilkie now. He cleared his throat and tugged on the cuffs of his shirt. He licked his lips, then started speaking in a voice so soft that Karlin and Weberman both strained forward in their chairs.

"This concerns Molly and Tad, gentlemen," he said. "My records show there was an interval of fourteen months between the times of their adoptions."

"Okay. So what?" Weberman was looking increasingly manic.

"It is important that you know they share a rare congenital heart ailment. It came to light only a few months ago . . ."

"Heart disease?" Karlin reacted. "Is it fatal?"

"We're talking about a treatable condition. It's a condition that manifests itself in children in their mid- to late teens. Medication is required, of course. I repeat, this is not life-threatening."

"I'm still on a different page," Weberman said. "This involves both kids? Why both kids?"

Wilkie remained silent for a moment, as though hesitant about disclosing the rest of his information. Eric peered at him impatiently, then at the others. "The answer to your question, Jake, is very simple," Eric said. "Molly and Tad happen to be brother and sister. Same mother. Same father."

"Born out of wedlock, of course," Wilkie put in softly.

Weberman and Karlin were both speechless, their faces pale, hands shaking. "I had no idea," Karlin said. "Jake, did you have even the vaguest . . . ?"

"We have a little problem here," Weberman said abruptly. "These two kids, they're . . . like, bonded. In fact, they've probably been intimate," Weberman said. "Let's own up to the mess we have here."

"Not my Molly," Karlin sputtered. "She's only sixteen and . . ."

"They're fucking. They've been fucking for at least a year."

Wilkie sagged in his chair. Karlin looked apoplectic. "And you," he said, pointing at Wilkie. "You've been selling us sick children . . ."

"Not true," Wilkie retorted. "In fact, the mother of these children is in perfect health. This condition skips a generation. There was no sign of any of this until recently when another of her children . . ."

"Another!" Karlin shouted. "What is she . . . a baby factory?"

Wilkie looked offended. "She is from a deprived background," he said. "She has had four children is all, and she has put three of them up for adoption."

"And you're making millions from this breeder and others like her."

"This is not a productive line of discourse," Eric put in.

"There are important issues that have been raised here." Weberman leaned forward, pointing a finger toward Eric. "Yeah, but look who's raising them. Why do we have to hear all this from the studio consigliere? Is the studio trying to grasp some leverage from this mess?"

Wilkie was shaking his head. "I thought we'd explained that," he offered. "I'd placed a child with Mr. Hoffman as well. Since I had no way of finding either Mr. Karlin or Mr. Weberman—fifteen years is a long time—I decided to contact you through Mr. Hoffman at the studio, even though his child does not share this condition."

But Bert Karlin heard none of this. He was staring at Weberman and he looked stricken. "Those kids . . . if they're involved with each other—" he started, then stopped. "Holy shit! Brother and sister. Your kid, Jake—I've always told you he was a wild kid. Out of control. He's taken advantage of Molly and now . . ."

"I am not a professional social worker," Wilkie said. "But my advice would be to sit them down together, particularly if they are that close. Lay out the information. They are old enough to understand the implications."

"My wife will go fucking bonkers," Karlin said.

"Together? How can we do it together?" Weberman said.

"For one thing, the two of you have to start communicating," Eric said.

The veins in Weberman's neck were bulging. "This devious prick has been cutting my movie behind my back," he said, pointing to Karlin.

Karlin bolted like he'd been struck by lightning. "You showed your cut to two critics before I even got to see it," he shot back. "You're trying to get the critics behind you when your cut isn't even locked."

"That's bullshit. Pure bullshit," Weberman raged.

"Kenny Turan confirmed it to me. He's the chief fucking critic of the *Los Angeles Times*, and you're sneaking screenings—"

"This isn't helping the cause," Eric cut in. "We've got a problem to address here about the children . . ."

"How am I supposed to deal with this guy when he's recutting my picture behind my back?" Weberman demanded.

Karlin sank back in his chair. "Look, Jake, we've got to deal with this thing. It's more important than a fucking movie."

"Some sanity at last," Eric said.

"We need a consensus here," Wilkie said.

A momentary silence settled over the room. Both Karlin and Weberman stared at the floor. "I'll call Jake tomorrow," Karlin said finally. "We'll talk."

"Okay by me," Jake Weberman said.

"I'm returning to Salt Lake City," Wilkie said. "But if you feel I can help . . ."

"You've done enough," Karlin said. He rose to leave. Weberman was on his heels. They did not look at each other as they left the room.

When they were gone, Eric felt Wilkie's gaze. "I don't know how you deal with people like that," Wilkie said. "They are not . . . reasonable people."

"The movie business does not attract reasonable people," Eric responded, as he escorted Wilkie to the door.

Over the next two days, Eric tried to put this encounter out of his mind, but somehow he kept replaying fragments of it. Everything about it was discomfiting. Neither of the two fathers had reacted with the sort of empathy he felt the situation merited. Wilkie's persona, chilly and distanced, reinforced his instinctual dislike for this man to whom children were pawns in a business transaction. Most of all, however, Eric felt a pang of remorse about his own role. He was playing God. He was manipulating events to suit his own scenario. Perhaps he was worse than Wilkie.

He chose not to discuss his feelings with his wife, Linda. In recent years Linda had resolutely avoided any mention that their daughter, Kimberly, also had been adopted. Eric understood the reason for her silence: A marriage counselor had stupidly advised her years earlier that Eric had resented their decision to adopt, that he felt guilt because his sperm count was insufficient to have children of his own. This was abject nonsense, Eric felt. He had long since accepted his inadequacies as a donor and, in view of that, had favored adopting Kimberly. Indeed, the adoption had served its prime purpose in keeping their marriage together, though his wife's controlling nature, her need to manipulate every situation, still grated on him.

Two nights after the meeting, Linda had started talking about her feelings toward adoption for the first time in years. They were having dinner at Le Dome with another couple,

Marvin and Ethel Wurtzel, also attorneys, when Marvin started relating details of a grim case that had taken up much of his day. A client of his, a top agent named Billy Chasin, had just adopted a baby girl when the baby's mother suddenly reversed herself and demanded that the child be returned. "Billy and his wife refused to give the baby back," Marvin explained. "He says, 'I don't care what it takes to buy her off, I don't care if we have to leave the country, that baby doesn't go back to the mother.'"

"That's always been my worst nightmare," Linda put in.

"Surely you explained to Billy that he's got no rights," Eric said.

"He won't listen to me," Marvin replied.

"I'm just amazed this doesn't happen more often," Ethel Wurtzel said, nibbling on a roll. "Everybody in this town is adopting. They don't want to take the time from their careers to have a family. Suddenly they're in their forties and it's too late."

"Have you guys seen the new Jim Carrey movie?" Eric asked, desperately trying to divert the conversation. No one seemed to hear him.

"Ethel makes a good point," Marvin said. "We decided our careers came first. Besides, most of the adoptions in this town are handled by two or three lawyers. It wouldn't surprise me if these kids came from a small group of breeders in Utah."

"Our Kimberly has meant the world to us," Linda said, all but swallowing her words.

Eric had been frantically signaling the waiter, who came

over finally, pad in hand, ready to take their orders. Once the ordering was finished, Marvin started talking about other litigation he had just filed.

The next morning, Eric was in a meeting when he was informed that Bert Karlin was on the phone. His news was not what Eric wanted to hear. Karlin said that he and Jake Weberman had met and had agreed that it should be Eric who would meet with the two kids, Molly and Tad. Shocked, Eric argued that this was not appropriate, but Karlin persisted. "Jake and I agree on this. This itself is a minor miracle," he explained. "If you break the news to the kids, it will sound official. You've got credibility. You've got to make them take the medical stuff seriously. Most important, you can find out whether they're . . . involved. Do you think they'd give Jake or me a straight answer? We're their parents, for chrissake. Parents never get a straight answer. You started this thing, Eric. The ball's in your court."

"Look, I'm just a lawyer. It's not my place . . ."

"The kids see you as an authority figure. You're someone important, not just a parent. They'll listen. Besides, Jake and I—we could never bring it off. We'd get into a fight before we could even broach the question."

"I don't want to get involved," Eric protested.

But he was trapped and he knew it. Over the next couple of days he talked with psychologists specializing in adolescent behavior. He rehearsed his presentation, plotted out possible replies and questions. He then made one final call to Karlin in the hope of eliciting a last-minute reprieve, but with no luck.

Indeed, Karlin was even vaguely intimidating. Eric under-stood the subtext. Bert was basically saying, "If you want me to play ball, then you'd better play ball." Bert Karlin was a tough hombre—that much Eric understood all too well.

That Thursday afternoon, Molly Karlin and Tad Weber-man were picked up at the end of the school day by a studio limousine and driven to Eric's sprawling Spanish revival house on Starlight Terrace. They were ushered into the den, offered soft drinks and cookies. They seemed to have no notion as to the purpose of their visit. Indeed, by the time Eric entered the room carrying a legal folder, the two kids seemed a little bored.

Though he'd rehearsed his lines, Eric felt ill at ease. He offered his hand to each of the kids as though starting a busi-ness meeting. Molly's hand was cold and clammy. Tad seemed indifferent.

"I know you're wondering what all this is about," Eric started out. "Let me just explain, I am here as a friend of the family, of both your families. As you know, my day job is that of executive vice president in charge of business affairs at Warner Brothers. This meeting has nothing to do with studio business. I want to be sure you understand that."

"Then why are we here?" Tad's tone was defiant and Eric found himself taking an instant dislike to him. Tad was a big-boned kid with stringy blond hair and a broad, Midwestern face. His piercing gaze focused unrelentingly on this stranger. He wore a Los Angeles Lakers T-shirt and baggy tan jeans. Seated across the room, Molly was a slender, almost frail-looking girl with pale skin and close-cropped blond hair. If Tad looked defiant, Molly seemed needy.

"There are several reasons you are here," Eric continued in his methodical, legalistic voice, as though relating the contents of a deal memo. "Let me emphasize once again that I am here at your parents' request."

"Then why aren't they here?" Molly said.

"That will become clear as we move along," Eric said. "I am going to give each of you a packet of medical material that will explain a condition you share. It is a congenital heart ailment. It is treatable. It is not life-threatening. The only important item to remember is that it requires medical attention. That means you see a doctor, get an examination and start a program of medication." Eric brought forth some papers and put them on the table before him. "Are there any questions?"

Both kids were exchanging looks of apprehension. "You're telling us that we both have this thing?" Tad asked.

"That's correct."

"How come? I mean, both of us?"

Eric sucked in his breath. "Because you are brother and sister, that's why." Molly turned white and fell silent. Tad flushed, tried to reply, but his words collided in an incoherent sputter.

"I realize this is a sensitive area and I don't want to upset you—that sounds stupid, so forgive me. Let's just say, you share the same mother. Probably the same father. That makes you siblings."

"I don't believe you," Tad said in a hoarse whisper.

"Shut up, Tad," Molly said. "He's trying to help us. Or something."

"So now there's gonna be a big drumroll and you're gonna reveal the identity of our real parents?" Tad said. "Is that it? 'Cause I can tell you now, I don't want to know. They dumped me years ago, so why should I care who they are or where they live?"

Molly stared at Tad, then at Eric. "Is that why we're here? Some big show-and-tell?"

Eric felt a sudden flash of heat. His brow was damp. He had run lots of tough meetings during his career and had trained himself to remain detached. Yet now, with these ridiculous kids he barely knew, he was sweating up a storm.

"I don't know the names of your birth parents or where they live or anything," Eric said, choosing his words carefully. "The reason your parents asked me to take this meeting is that they have a specific area of concern." Eric drew another breath. "They felt that it would be easier for an outsider—that is, someone outside the family—to explore . . ."

"You want to know if we're sleeping together. That's it, isn't it?" Eric felt Tad's angry gaze. Molly turned away, as though refusing to acknowledge this conversation was taking place.

"That's one way of putting it," Eric said in a flat voice.

"Well, what do you think? We've been hooked up for two years. We do our homework together. We hang together. We go to class together . . ."

"I just don't see that it's anyone's business . . ." Molly was having trouble arraying her words.

"We usually get it on twice a week," Tad said, his voice filled with contempt. "Two Saturdays ago my parents were in Vegas so we basically screwed all day. This morning she gave me a hand job after French class 'cause she saw me sticking out like a tent pole, but I suppose that doesn't count."

"Tad, why don't you just shut up," Molly said.

"Hey, this guy wants to know about our sex life so he can tell our folks. I'm just trying to be helpful."

"My purpose here is to be sure you understand that having sex with a sibling is a crime in the state of California. It is known as incest. By admitting these acts to me, you are placing yourself in a dangerous situation."

"That means you're gonna rat on us?"

"No, it means this: I'm going to give you the name and phone number of a family counselor. I strongly urge you to seek her help. Your relationship cannot continue on its present basis. Do you understand?"

"Are you gonna rat on us?" Tad had half risen from his chair.

"My purpose here—"

"Stop repeating that . . . !"

"Just for the record, Tad, I don't like you, either."

Tad was on his feet now, tears rolling down his cheeks. Molly moved to him, shoved him back into his chair, then turned to Eric. "Look, Mr. Hoffman, I know you mean well. It's just— Tad and I love each other. We want to be together always."

Tad sat staring at the floor, utterly disconsolate. Eric paced across the room. "I feel like a complete prick," he mumbled, as though to himself.

"What do you think we should do?" Molly asked.

"I'm not good at playing God," Eric said. "I'm just a lawyer. What the hell do I know? Ask your parents."

"I don't know my father any better than I know you," Tad said, still staring at the floor.

"We love our parents, mind you," Molly put in. "We appreciate all they have done for us. The cars, the schools, the clothes. They've been very generous and all. It's just that . . . well, there's a distance."

"So what should we do?" Tad asked again. "You're paid to have the big ideas."

"I'd switch schools. I'd try to see each other only when other people are around. I'd try to lessen the risk of . . . of getting too close again. The law's the law. Besides, if you had children . . ."

"We understand all that," Molly said.

Eric faced them both now. "Look, I'm terribly sorry . . . That's all I can say. I feel just awful."

"So do we." Tad rose, took Molly's hand and silently walked toward the front door. Eric followed them outside, saw the studio car awaiting them. Molly climbed in, waving tentatively to Eric, who waved back. The car drove off. Eric returned to his den and poured himself a drink. Suddenly he realized there were tears on his face.

For days, Eric could not take his mind off his meeting, despite all the pressures of work. He heard nothing from

Molly and Tad, and that did not surprise him. Meanwhile, the impasse over *Crossroads* seemed to be resolved. Jake Weberman ran his cut for Karlin, who made some suggestions but generally approved. Karlin then ran his "rogue" version, and Jake, while hating it, nonetheless appropriated several of its ideas. Their joint version was then run for Derek Kirsh and several of his underlings, who made still further suggestions, changed a few music cues, but generally gave it their approval. Kirsh phoned Eric after the screening and congratulated him for settling the dispute between the producer and director. This was the first time, to Eric's knowledge, that Derek had ever uttered a word of praise to a colleague.

A day after the screening, Eric encountered Jake Weberman in the executive dining room of the commissary. Jake was eating with an agent and seemed cheerful.

"Congratulations," Eric said matter-of-factly. "Everyone's very happy with the film."

"The early tracking looks great," Weberman said. "We may have a blockbuster on our hands."

"Any word from the kids?"

Jake seemed at a loss. "The kids? . . . Well, I really don't know."

"Don't know?"

"They're not here. Didn't Karlin tell you? I mean, what happened is that they've run away."

"Have you called in the cops?"

"Well, in view of all the . . . complications . . . well, we thought it best to hire a private investigator."

"And?"

"And nothing so far. I'll keep you posted."

Eric did not hear anything further from either Weberman or Karlin. A day later a handwritten letter arrived at his office. It was from Molly and was written in a childlike scrawl. "Dear Mr. Hoffman," the letter stated. "I know you tried to help. I just wanted to thank you. Afterward all we got was yelling and screaming from our parents, so we decided to go away. I wanted you to know we are fine, Tad has a job, so do I and we are being careful. Please tell our parents not to look for us. Thanks again. Molly. P.S. If we ever decide to have children, we will adopt them."

Eric was about to fax the letter to Karlin and Weberman. Then he thought better of it. He planted a quick kiss on the note, then tossed it in his wastebasket.

He left his office early that evening and took his daughter to the ballet. She seemed as pleased as she was surprised.

The Neighbors II

An emergency meeting of the Starlight Terrace Neigh-borhood Association was initially scheduled at Todd Plover's place, but directors received a last-minute e-mail informing them that Marty Gellis would instead play host. They were not surprised. In the three weeks following their past meeting, rumors had circulated that Plover, their pres-ident, had left his wife and moved to Venice Beach, but the reasons given were contradictory. That intrigue was surely the reason why all eight directors were in atten-dance at Marty Gellis's elegant Tudor, a formal and impos-ing home that looked ill at ease in its rustic setting, with the thickets of brush and ivy encroaching from all sides.

"I've got a six *a.m.* call tomorrow," Denise Turley said, sinking into a sofa. "Can we move things along quickly?"

"Denise's dailies are so hot, everyone at the studio is

buzzing," Marty Gellis said. "This will be an automatic Oscar nomination."

"Stop selling, Marty," Denise admonished.

"Let's get to the business at hand," Plover said. "We have to vote to refile the lawsuit against Barry Gal."

"I don't understand why our first suit was rejected," Nancy Mendoza said.

"There was a technical mistake in the original filing, or at least the court thought so," said Eric Hoffman.

"The guy's movie shoot is a bigger pain than his building plan," said Marty Gellis. "His crew promised to shut down by nightfall, and they were still rolling at midnight. Who could sleep?"

"When I drove home from dinner they were filming their chase scene," said Sidney Garman. "They almost drove me off the road."

"Barry Gal's making it dangerous to live here," said Denise Turley.

"I'm sorry I ever complained about his parties," said Nancy Mendoza. "I wish he'd go back to parties and forget about movies."

"Then let's file two suits," Todd Plover suggested. "One to block his construction and one to cease and desist with the movie."

Tom Patch was shaking his head in exasperation. "We've got to stop this motherfucker," he said. "My new bride is a tree hugger and she'll freak if she sees anyone cutting down the eucalyptus grove."

"I can't promise immediate results about the movie shoot," Eric Hoffman said. "Knowing Barry Gal, he's bribed the right people and gotten the permits, but we can try. On the other litigation, we have a good fighting chance to stop him cold."

"Let's take another vote then," Plover said.

"Oops." The interruption came from Sidney Garman.

"What's the 'oops' about?" asked Denise Turley.

"This Barry Gal guy made an offer on one of my scripts. A big offer. Like two million. Does that mean I shouldn't vote?"

"Have you accepted the offer?" Eric Hoffman asked.

"The auction is still going on."

"I guess that's a conflict. Just like with Marty and Eric at the last meeting," Plover said.

"The son of a bitch is buying our board," Denise Turley said. "That's what's going on."

"We've still got five people to vote," said Elizabeth Donahue. "Let's vote quick before someone else gets an offer."

Five hands shot up. Todd Plover looked surprised. "I haven't even posed the question."

"Motion's passed," said Gellis. "Refile the fucking suit."

"It'll be done," Hoffman said.

"Can I go home now?" asked Denise Turley.

"There's one other matter," Plover said, running a hand through his perfectly groomed brown hair. "This is the last meeting I'm presiding over. As you may know, I've moved from the neighborhood . . ."

"We've heard," said Nancy Mendoza. "We're really sorry to lose you."

"And I'm sorry to leave you all."

"So it's none of my goddamn business, except that I am a screenwriter and I'm terminally curious . . ." Sidney Garman's voice trailed off.

"You want to know why?" Plover said.

"We've all heard rumors," said Denise Turley. "If you want to say something, fine. If not, who gives a shit?"

"I suppose you know that I've moved in with a new partner," Todd Plover explained. "This time a guy partner."

There was silence. Then Marty Gellis clasped his wineglass. "Here's to your happiness," he said, taking a hasty sip. "You sure had me fooled, kid. I never figured you for one of my tribe."

"I'm afraid I fooled everyone," Plover said. "Even myself."

"This horny old faggot is jealous," Denise Turley said, digging an elbow into Marty Gellis's ribs.

"And Megan? Is she all right?" asked Nancy Mendoza.

"She's pissed off. She's got a right to be pissed off. She's going to stay in our house, of course. It will be hers if she wants it."

"You know we all wish you well, Todd," said Eric Hoffman. "We want the best for you."

"I'll miss the 'hood," said Todd Plover. "I really will."

"I don't think you'll miss Barry Gal," Elizabeth Donahue said.

"He's the neighbor from hell," said Marty Gellis.

"We can't evict him, but our lawsuits may give him pause," Eric Hoffman said.

"Find a place for him in Venice, Todd," Tom Patch said.

"Barry Gal is like this anonymous creature who keeps buying things," Sidney Garman said. "He's like the Starlight Terrace version of Viacom and Vivendi and all these other faceless corporations that have bought up our industry."

"Look who's talking," Marty Gellis said. "I read in the trades you sold a script for over a million dollars. At this rate, you'll be as rich as Barry Gal."

"I've had a streak of luck," Sidney Garman said.

Todd Plover was on his feet. "I'd better get out of here," he said. "Maybe Eric will take over as interim president while you decide on a new one. I hope you solve your problems with Barry Gal. Sorry to duck out on you."

"Stay well," said Nancy Mendoza.

"Thank you," Plover said, even as he was shutting the door behind him. When he was gone the other directors sat quietly for a few moments. "I always thought he was too cute to be straight," Denise Turley said finally.

"They were a nice couple," said Nancy Mendoza.

"On that note . . ." Eric Hoffman gave everyone a quick wave, then headed for the door.

Tom Patch started to follow him out, then turned. "How do you wake up one morning, stare at yourself in the mirror and say, 'I'm gay'?"

"I assure you, you'll never find out," Marty Gellis said.

Now heads turned as Eric Hoffman's voice came booming at them from the front door. "You've all got to see this," he called. "If you think the cop chases were bad, take a look at what Barry Gal's crew is shooting tonight!"

Sidney Garman was the first to the door. He took in the situation and started to laugh. "My God, we've descended totally into schlockville!" he exploded.

"I think I'll move," said Denise Turley, standing behind him.

Arrayed before them was the movie crew, some fifty or so in number. Illuminated in the harsh light were two figures, a man wearing a police uniform and a woman who seemed to be totally naked. He had her handcuffed and was coaxing her into his police car, but she was resisting. The actor dressed as a cop finally slapped her harshly across her butt. She wheeled and bit his hand, whereupon he yelled and slapped her harder.

The director, standing behind the camera, shouted, "Cut, let's do it again."

"No fucking way," bleated the naked actress, shivering in the cold night air.

Watching from Marty Gellis's doorstep, the neighbors looked aghast. "I'm embarrassed to be in show business," Elizabeth Donahue said.

"I'm going to bring that young lady a blanket," Nancy Mendoza said. "They're freezing her butt."

"I think she's more worried about the slapping than the freezing," said Sidney Garman.

"We've got to figure a way of running Barry Gal out of

town," said Denise Turley. "Even if we have to get him kid-napped."

"I'd prefer to think there are other ways," Eric Hoffman said.

"Find them," said Elizabeth Donahue.

Dangerous Company

The instant Dan Carillo awakened, a menu of options flashed onto his consciousness as though he were peering at a computer screen. He could leap out of bed, pull on his clothes and make a run for it. That way their encounter would remain impersonal, which would be cool because they surely would never see each other again. Option Two was that he would roll over. His fingers had accidentally brushed her naked bottom so he knew she was there, her back toward him, still asleep and, like him, utterly wasted. Maybe her eyes would flutter open, there would be a quick exchange, he would thank her and then make his exit. Of course, there was also Option Three: She would awaken, they would kiss and replay the previous night, then linger over coffee, perhaps take each other's phone numbers and e-mail addresses and vow to get together. Option Three would be a nice option because, after all, it was Christmas morning and they were together, and yet alone. That much had become clear when they met at the party.

He took a breath, relieved, because he could now remember her name. She'd been introduced as Elizabeth Donahue. She was a vivid wisp of a woman, barely five feet tall, perhaps in her early thirties, but what he remembered most were her eyes. Her eyes seemed to speak to him: They said, Yeah, I get it, you're funny and you're full of shit, even as her small mouth curled into an ironic smile. He was taken by surprise when she invited him home to Starlight Terrace after the party, surprised also by her lavish, sprawling home. But then their host at the Christmas Eve party, Dr. Sidney Zimmerman, seemed to collect unpredictable divorcées. In fact, he collected all sorts of types. They were his patients, most of them, as was Dan, and at his parties he mixed them skillfully. There'd always be a scattering of stars and directors so as to achieve an appropriate balance of glitz and wannabes, of people looking and people wanting not to be looked at. They were good parties, and Dan came to most of them, grateful to be invited since he was, after all, a wannabe, a young actor getting bit parts and praying for callbacks. Dr. Zimmerman's wife, Sylvia, had confided to him, in so many words, that there was always a need for a handsome young stud who could smile at the divorcées and make nice and maybe go home with one, though Elizabeth, in that respect, was his first, at least from Dr. Zimmerman's parties—the first time he had actually been propositioned. To be sure, hers was hardly a textbook proposition. They had been drinking margaritas and both were swackered and she had simply said, "Let's go to my place, Dan. Think of me as a Christmas present."

Deciding on Option Two now, Dan turned over gingerly and found himself staring into a pair of eyes, fully awake and utterly expressionless. "Who are you and why are you here?" she said softly.

"Good morning, Elizabeth."

"I don't do things like this."

"Merry Christmas. You're my Christmas present, remember."

"I have a terminal headache. I need coffee and aspirin." She started to get out of bed, then stopped. "I am also buck naked. You go first."

"I am also naked, I also have a headache and I also have a major erection, so I would appreciate it if you'd go first."

There was a trace of a grin on her face, which wiped away quickly as she climbed out of bed and darted toward the bathroom. At the bathroom door, she froze. "This is stupid. We fucked all night and now we're bashful. Get out of bed."

He climbed out of bed. She peered at him, bemused. "You can use the other bathroom. Turn right down the hall."

After he had dressed, he found her in the kitchen sipping coffee and smoking. A second cup sat across the table, with an aspirin beside it. She was reading an e-mail, and he could also hear a fax machine humming. "Christmas greetings?" he asked.

"You might say so."

Dan seated himself. The coffee was strong. "At least it's Christmas morning, the worst is behind us."

She looked up. "You mean, this is the good part? Two total strangers, hung over, trying to reconstruct what happened last night?"

He popped the aspirin. "I enjoyed what happened. Sorry you didn't."

"Don't put words in my mouth." She rose and crossed the room. She looked sexy in her baggy shirt and clinging jeans, hair still askew. "You want a croissant? It's two days old."

"Just coffee's fine. Walking in here, I noticed—no Christmas decorations. Nothing. That's unusual for a good Catholic girl."

"What makes you think I'm a good Catholic girl?"

"Elizabeth Donahue. That's you, right?"

She tore off a piece of the crumbly croissant and ate it. "So I'm Catholic, am I? And I don't have any Christmas decorations. Have you done any more detective work on me?"

"Well, you're neat, that's for sure. You even iron your panties."

"Have you been going through my drawers, too?"

"No, your panty drawer was open. Just happened to look." He stood up and stretched. "You've got a great place here. Starlight Terrace. Famous place. Million-dollar homes. I'd figure you got an excellent settlement."

"You think you're good at this?"

"Hey, I'm an actor. That means I'm not very smart, but I have intuition. At least that's what my manager tells me."

Elizabeth bit off another piece of croissant. "So is this why you picked me up last night? You're into rich divorcées."

Dan drained his coffee. "Nope. I liked you. I liked that you didn't need to be the center of attention. I liked that you weren't talking about deals, like the other people at Dr. Zimmerman's. It was like a meat market there. I learned that Kevin Spacey's price is now twelve million against five percent of the gross. Sean Penn gets only two million and net, but on his last flick he got a rollback at fifty million, whatever that means." He poured himself another cup. "Besides, you picked me up, remember?"

Elizabeth sat across from him. "And we owe all this to Dr. Zimmerman. How long have you been seeing him?"

"Just a year. My manager told me about him. His head is a showbiz history book. I go to him for a nosebleed and he tells me about Brando's deviated septum."

"He's not exactly Mr. Discretion. It's one thing to tell me Gary Cooper had a peptic ulcer. Couple weeks ago he also confided that George Hamilton had crabs."

A grin creased Dan's face. Their eyes met. "So do you want me to leave? I feel like my parking meter's run out."

"It's just that I've got things to do. I've got to scroll through my e-mail . . ." Dan got to his feet. Elizabeth turned toward him. "Don't," she said.

"Don't what?"

"You don't have to leave. Of course, if you have an appointment . . ."

"Who makes appointments on Christmas Day?"

"Look, I'm sorry . . . I'm not good at morning afters. Why don't we go out, get some brunch? What the hell?"

Dan smiled. "Yeah, what the hell. But while you read your e-mail, maybe I can take a shower. I'm a little gamey."

"You know where the bathroom is. There's a towel . . . ?"

"Yeah, there's a towel."

The aspirin kicked in even as the hot water pounded on his scalp and shoulders. Dan realized he suddenly was feeling okay. In fact, he felt great. She had made him feel great. She had scared him at first. When they got to her house her eyes had gone blurry and he feared the booze had gotten to her. It had happened to him before—"I get crazy if I don't sleep," one girl told him before she conked out. And then there was the proverbial headache—that had happened, too, but Elizabeth had simply started taking off her clothes. In bed she seemed passive, so Dan had decided he would go slow, kissing her breasts and caressing her ass and just holding her. He could not recall the precise moment when he realized that he had gauged her wrong, that she was not the quiet, passive lover but was, in fact, utterly in control. She was riding him fiercely, and after both had come, she was still after him like a tigress, mouth engulfing him, fingers probing him everywhere. She had thoroughly exhausted him, but even as he fell asleep, he peered at her furtively, still surprised by her ardor.

When he had toweled off and dressed, he returned to the kitchen but found it empty. He called for her but got no answer. He walked into the living room, which was a vast space dominated by two oversized white sofas, then into the dining room, with its ornate antique table. He was headed for the kitchen again when they all but collided. She was still in jeans but dressier ones and wore a red silk blouse under a green cashmere sweater that had a Prada label sticking out the top.

"You look very Christmassy, for someone who doesn't 'do' Christmas," he offered.

"A token gesture," she said.

He followed Elizabeth back into the kitchen.

"It's amazing what aspirin and a shower can do," he said. "Not to mention a chance meeting with a beautiful stranger."

"That's not a very fresh line."

"Hey, I'm an actor. Actors need writers. Especially me. Especially now."

"Hey, I'm not *that* tough . . ."

"No, no, it's not about you. I don't want to burden you with my troubles, but I just tested for the lead on a soap. That's where the writers come in."

Elizabeth stared at him and froze, but he didn't notice as he continued his peroration. "I mean, the lines I had—they were totally lame. The network's going to judge me not on my performance but on those lines. That's what's really bumming me out. I'm kind of hanging by my thumbs."

Elizabeth shook her head and turned. "I think we both need some food. I know just the place." Dan looked after her, relieved.

The ride down to the Strip from the Hollywood Hills took only ten minutes. Dan marveled at the expert way Elizabeth guided her speeding Porsche, which seemed suffused with that leathery "new car" smell.

Only a few tables at Hugo's were occupied and no one was on hand even to seat them. It was the post-Christmas lull. She headed for a window table that looked out on Santa Monica

Boulevard. It was usually clogged with traffic but all but deserted at the moment.

When a waiter finally materialized, she ordered a mushroom omelet and he the French toast with sausages. The waiter was a tall, handsome surfer type with a swath of rusty blond hair. He showed a flicker of recognition as he took Dan's order.

"Friend of yours?" she asked.

Dan shook his head. "Another actor. We've read for the same parts a coupla times. He's pretty good until he has to read with an actress. That blows his cover. He goes swishy."

"Pity. He's a good-looking guy."

"Waiting tables—every actor's basic profession. You think you're getting somewhere, then suddenly you're tapped out and you're waiting tables again."

"But you, Dan—you're past that. You don't have to worry . . ."

He looked at her. "How do you know?"

"Know what?"

"How I'm doing."

"Oh, shit," she said, reaching into her purse, fumbling for a cigarette.

"They're going to tell you to put it out."

"Then I'll put it out. Look, Dan, there's something I've got to tell you . . ."

"This isn't going to be one of those scenes where one lover tells the other about an arcane sexual disease, is it?"

"It isn't a joke. I feel terrible."

"About what? You've been wonderful."

"You can't smoke in here." The voice came from two tables over. It was a whiny, fey voice belonging to a middle-aged queen who was waving at them. Elizabeth stubbed out her cigarette with a quick, irritated gesture. "I'm sorry," the queen said. "I'd like to smoke myself. In fact, why don't we both light up?" He brightened, then took out a cigarette. Elizabeth did the same.

Dan's eyes were boring into her. "So what's this about?" he said.

Elizabeth sucked in some air, stared at her cigarette, then put it back in her purse. "I'm not the person you think I am. I wish I were. I don't know what I wish."

"Now I'm totally confused."

"I'm not a rich divorcée. What I am is . . . oh, shit. I work at a network. That's the reason for the faxes and e-mails you saw me reading. They weren't Christmas greetings, they were the overnights."

"Okay, I can deal with that. It's a power thing . . ."

"It gets worse. I am vice president for daytime programming at ABC. *Daytime*, get it?"

"Got it. I told you, actors aren't very smart."

"And I saw your tests. I mean, I didn't put it all together until we sat down at this table. Don't ask me why. Suddenly I realized it was you and those were your tests. Shit."

He froze, even as the waiter plunked down their omelet and French toast. "You want some coffee? Orange juice?" he asked. There was no response. The waiter looked from Dan to Elizabeth, then back to Dan. "Is this some sort of zen thing?" he asked.

"Coffee. Yes, coffee, please," Elizabeth muttered.

"You've seen my test for the soap?" Dan's voice was a hoarse whisper.

"I saw it two weeks ago. That's why I thought you looked vaguely familiar at the party, but you know how it is at Dr. Zimmerman's—everyone looks vaguely familiar. Then when we were in the kitchen, you started talking about the soap and . . . Shit! I don't believe this is happening!"

"Do you think I did okay? I mean, Zak is a terrific part. He's tough, he's romantic—I could play the hell out of him."

"You were fine. Just fine. But surely you realize how inappropriate this is. It's totally unprofessional of me . . . I mean, I'm fucking an actor who's up for a role in one of my shows."

"Okay. It's not exactly kosher, but who'll ever know?"

"I will know. That's bad enough."

"Look, I don't want to be tacky, Elizabeth, and I appreciate your sensitivity to this, but . . . well . . . I could be a great Zak. I mean, you don't want me to be waiting on tables and . . ."

"It's not just me. There are five of us who decide and the feeling was, frankly, you're too ethnic. We want to go in another direction. More Middle America."

Dan pushed his French toast away. "What does that mean, too ethnic?"

"The whole Italian shtick. I mean, you're terrific. The

producer of the show said you remind him of a young Al Pacino. But . . ."

"I'm not too ethnic. I mean, I just thought that was the look you'd want. Carillo isn't even my real name. I'm Dan Hansen. I'm from Minneapolis. It was my manager—she told me my career would move much faster if I went to longer hair and got a tan and, well, got ethnic. She said Middle American types weren't getting the roles this year. Is our fucking waiter working, for Chrissake?"

Their waiter was, in fact, towering over them. "Something wrong? Would you prefer something else?"

"It's us, not the food," Elizabeth explained. "Something's wrong with us."

The waiter retreated, perplexed. Elizabeth lit a cigarette, took a nervous puff, then stubbed it out angrily. "Look, Dan, I don't know what to tell you. I feel terrible. It's Christmas and I'm saying things you don't want to hear and they shouldn't be coming from me, anyway."

"Too ethnic! I never should have listened to my manager. No one I know listens to his manager."

"And I probably should not be telling you any of this."

"Look, I'm a big boy. I gotta know sometime. I've been hanging by my thumbs, like I said. Shit."

"I'm sorry, Dan."

"No, I'm sorry. Sorry about all of this. You know how delusional I am? When we sat down I had this fantasy that we could have brunch, then go back to your place. Maybe spend the day together in bed."

"That would have been nice." She took out her purse. "Look, let me get the check at least." She seemed suddenly very businesslike.

"Buying breakfast for the starving actor?"

"Nothing like that."

"Can I ask you just one question, Elizabeth?"

She gave him a wistful glance. "It's wrong for us to be seeing each other."

"That wasn't what I wanted to ask."

"What?"

"Now that you know I'm really Dan Hansen, not Dan Carillo, do you think I could test for Zak one more time?"

She looked across the table at him and shook her head dolefully. Then she planted a kiss on his cheek, put a twenty on the table and headed resolutely for the door. She did not look back. Had she done so, she could have seen Dan calmly grasping his full plate of French toast and sausage, and turning it upside down on the table. He then stared somberly out the window, his eyes following Elizabeth Donahue as she climbed into her car. "Great ass," he told himself. "Also great car."

Power Play

The first thing Justin Braun liked to do when he checked into the Hotel du Cap was to summon up a glass of champagne, repair to the balcony of his suite, then just stand and stare. The sights were familiar and reinforcing: the expanse of manicured lawn, the stone pathways, the soothing symmetry of the gardens. Perched at the edge of the Mediterranean was the stolid chateau called Eden Roc that housed the restaurant, its pool nestled to one side, and the grand yachts skimming across the bay in the background. To Justin, all this was beyond imposing: It was magisterial. It bespoke serious money, old money. And now this would be his new world. He had defied the nettlesome predictions of his critics. He would not become a prisoner of the past. He had done what he does best: reinvented himself. He had conjured up a new Justin Braun.

Justin drained his glass and returned to his room. There

were calls to be made, deals to be cemented. It was all in his grasp now, that much he knew. Closing on the Chateau de la Vaucennes had been laborious, but he had anticipated all that. The negotiation had been in progress for six months now. He had mastered the tortuous convolutions of French law, buttered all the outstretched bureaucratic palms, bestowed a bonus on the "notaire" who had helped him secure the title. With it all, the price of the transaction had escalated thirty percent since the negotiation had begun. He was now paying $11.8 million for his new estate in the south of France and he knew he was overpaying. But the chateau represented more than a mere residence. It would be his new headquarters, the salon to which Europe's reigning corporate hierarchs would be attracted. It would be the seedbed of his new empire. As such, it was worth all the excruciating negotiation. It was his future.

On his way from the airport, Justin had instructed his chauffeur to drive by the chateau so he could remind himself that it was not the product of his errant imagination. The gates were locked, and the graceful seventeenth-century structure was shrouded in mist, but he could see it was real, and he understood, more than ever, that it was a world-class showplace.

Sprawling over twenty-four acres, the Chateau de la Vaucennes had been the prized possession first of royalty, then of wealthy landowners and, most recently, of major corporate wealth. Its ornate public rooms bespoke their history, with their balustraded balconies, mullioned windows and diamond-patterned marble floors. A supposedly priceless eighteenth century Piedmontese fresco adorned the dining room, which

could seat a hundred guests. Fine statuary loomed everywhere, and outside there was a barn and stables and a splen-
didly rococo swimming pool, replete with encroaching sea
serpents. And this all now belonged to Justin Braun, who had
come of age in a little tract pillbox in the middle of the San
Fernando Valley and who'd pulled down two after-school jobs
because his father kept getting fired from his own. Even as a
boy, Justin had learned that nothing would come to him without a struggle and hence was prepared to fight twice as hard.
The day before his bar mitzvah he'd discovered his father had
failed to come up with the money for his suit: He could feel
the rabbi's scorn when he turned up in a polo shirt. Justin
liked to tell that story to interviewers in later years. He
wanted everyone to know that "the most powerful man in
Hollywood," as he had come to be known, had not had anything handed to him. The industry was now full of soft rich
kids, Harvard M.B.A.'s and law school graduates, but they
were not of his ilk. He was "old school," and proud of it.

But that world was now in his past. No longer did he have
to respond to the ego demands of superstar clients. No more
would he get midnight calls from film locations or from police
stations. No longer did he have to fret about other people's
career crises. He'd faced career crises of his own and survived
them. And now he was going to prove his mettle to the world
yet again.

Justin saw it was six o'clock and his next appointment was
not until eight thirty P.M., when he was scheduled to have dinner with an unctuous Parisian attorney named Philippe

Verrier. In the past, Justin had introduced Verrier to important American clients, and now the Frenchman was returning the favor. If Verrier were properly motivated, Justin knew he could deliver important players from Canal Plus, France's pay TV oligopoly and others from the Berlusconi organization in Italy. These were organizations that would covet Justin's know-how of the American market and important media contacts. Some time during the evening, Justin also expected an update from his "notaire," Jacques le Doucet, who might have papers ready for signature. Le Doucet had said he might even drop by for a nightcap to celebrate the closing.

On impulse, Justin changed into his bathing suit and hurried down to the pool. A quick swim would energize him for his stultifying encounters, he reasoned.

There were several couples at the pool. Justin walked by a heavy-bosomed German woman who was grotesquely topless. A tanned French couple was smoking Gitanes and reading *Le Monde*. A boy-toy type stood poised on the diving board, clad in his sliver of blue spandex, flexing his abs. Justin grabbed the rail of the steps, leapt into the pool and immediately felt himself shriveling against the frigid water. The French did not believe in heating their pools, he remembered, even at the Hotel du Cap, and he felt as though his pulse had halted in midbeat. All right, he would start swimming briskly. He needed a jolt and this had done the job.

He was toweling himself at poolside when the waiter approached holding a mobile phone. "Pardon, monsieur," he said, apologizing for the intrusion.

"Hello," Justin barked into the phone.

"Is everything going okay?" The voice of his wife, Jodie, had a whiny lilt, even when merely posing a question.

"I've got it nailed," Justin said into the phone. "I'll be signing the final documents tonight or tomorrow."

"I had the plumber here for four hours. The pipes are backed up. I hate this place," she said.

"It's just a rental. For one year you can make do."

"I hate Starlight Terrace. It's tacky. Like its name."

"So you would have turned down the offer on our house? Think a moment, Jodie. A world-class director offers us eight million dollars for our house, which we know isn't worth half that much, and you'd tell him to fuck off?" Justin felt himself breaking into a sweat. No client, no matter how petulant or insulting, could get him as pissed off as she.

"Adam was very upset last night. I think he was crying."

"Probably trouble at school. He'll get over it."

"He read that story about you in *Esquire*. That's an awful story, Justin."

"He's a big boy. He's got to learn what it means to be in the public eye."

"Did you read it, Justin? It laid the whole collapse of the agency on you. It said your ego was out of control. That you betrayed your colleagues."

"So fuck 'em. Who cares what they write? I mean, why do you read that shit?"

"How can you not read it? Adam's friends even remind him about it."

"So why are you telling me this, Jodie? You want me to wave a magic wand and make it go away?"

"Everything was going so well for so long . . ."

"I'm going to hang up now, Jodie. I told you—I intend to change our lives. To leave all that shit behind us. So deal with the plumber and tell Adam to grow up and I'm hanging up now because I want to get ready for tonight. Good-bye."

Even as he punched "off," he felt a wave of relief. Ever since the problems had started at the agency, Jodie had been plunged into depression. But Justin did not believe in depression. He simply wouldn't abide it. He would decide exactly what he wanted his mood to be, exactly what thoughts would be allowed to invade his consciousness. That was his belief system. Self-control. It went beyond that: It was self-mastery. Jodie was a weak person; she could not understand.

The Verrier meeting cheered him, however. The Frenchman smoked four cigarettes and drank a $225 bottle of Clos de l'Église 1998, but he also said he could deliver Canal Plus as a client. That company, he said, was intent on shaking up its management philosophy and was persuaded that Justin could lead them to better times. The account could be worth 500,000 euros a year—just the sort of payday Justin had been seeking. There were other possibilities as well—a new French TV sports network, for example, and also a big advertising agency. To be sure, Verrier would elicit a substantial fee for delivering clients to Justin Braun's new consulting company, but his services would merit those rewards. When Justin had started up his agency, he had changed the rules as well. His first superstar clients paid only a 2½ percent commission, not the standard 10 percent mandated by established agencies. And Justin had dispensed tens of thousands of dollars in alleged legal fees to attorneys who'd sent new clients his way—fees that were in return for no services other than delivering talent. These were all appropriate start-up expenses, Justin felt, and Verrier would now be one of the lucky recipients.

It was 11 P.M. when Justin returned to his hotel. The robotic night concierge, immaculately groomed as always, handed him his key along with two messages. Jodie had called again—her normal drumbeat of calls. He decided to give himself a treat tonight and not return them. His hand was on the lift button when the second message froze him in his tracks. "Monsieur Litwin is waiting for you in the bar," it said. This was surely a joke. Not a funny joke, either. Probably the brainstorm of a former colleague who'd phoned the hotel from Los Angeles.

Justin hurried back to the concierge and held the message before him. "This message—it came in a phone call, right? A call from L.A.?"

The concierge looked baffled. "Non, monsieur. Monsieur Litwin—he is in the bar. He is your associate, non? I remember, when you both stayed here before there were big parties. And movie stars."

"Former associate," Justin growled under his breath, even as he found himself moving slowly toward the bar. He felt disoriented, forcibly redeployed to a different moment in time.

Four French businessmen were arguing a deal at one corner table in the bar. The lighting was, as always, dim. And seated in the opposite corner, alone, was Josh Litwin, who saw Justin now and rose to greet him. Justin felt an instant awkwardness. During their twenty years as partners at the agency, they had made a ritual of the big bear hug. It sent a message of solidarity to clients and colleagues. Whatever the tensions of the moment, nothing would wedge itself between Justin and Josh. That bond was key to their success. But there was no need to hug now. There was instead a safe handshake; four hands clasped, albeit briefly. Then both took their seats.

Justin saw the drink before him. "Someone already sitting here?"

"No, that's your sambuca," Josh said. "I ordered it for you. You always liked to end the night here with a sambuca, right?"

Justin started to respond, then caught himself. He took a sip, and stared across the table.

"So, what the hell? It's been, what, eighteen . . . twenty months?" Josh said.

"Yeah, something like that." Josh wore a casual sweater and jeans. His iron-gray hair was still close-cropped, his voice gravelly. At fifty, Josh still looked like the tough ex-Marine, but he was now the president of a movie company, a fact that Justin could never quite bring himself to acknowledge. Yet Josh had actually started to look the part—that much was clear.

"So we've dropped enough bucks in this place, right?" Josh said with a sort of clenched smile. "The party for Tom Cruise alone set us back six hundred and fifty thousand dollars. And we had to pay for Julia Roberts's yacht for four days to get her to attend."

"Yeah, and the owners here are real grateful types," Justin said. "I mean, the room they tried to give me this week was one I used to assign to Tom Cruise's fuckin' press agent. I had to fight to get my old suite."

"Hey, the Krauts still own this place, right?"

Justin nodded, then stared at his ex-partner again. "So what's with the surprise visit, Josh? I mean, what the fuck are you doing here?"

Josh shrugged. "I'm staying on my boat actually, but I had a business dinner at the Eden Roc, so I thought I'd stay for a nightcap. For old times' sake."

"So this is a chance meeting, is that it? Like, an accident?"

"I guess you'd call it that. For that matter, what brings you here, kiddo?"

"Also business. I'm buying a place nearby. Maybe you know that already."

"I heard rumblings that you might be moving here. Something like that," Josh said, as he signaled for another round. "Ready for seconds? You're a cheap date. Sambuca is only sixty dollars a shot while my pathetic cognac is a ninety-five-dollar hit."

"I'll go for another." Justin glanced around the room, then fixed his gaze on Josh again. "So every newspaper and magazine interview about you . . . they all seem to contain a knock on your ex- partner. If you believe what you read, you'd think old Josh has a chip on his shoulder."

"The fucking press. What can you do?"

"So these reporters . . . they're inventing it all?"

"Something like that. Hey, the two of us—we shared a fox-hole for twenty years. We won our share of battles, too."

The waiter delivered the new round. Justin noticed Josh's hands quivered slightly as he drained his cognac. "We were number one in town. Number one in the most competitive business there is," Justin said.

"I'll grant you that," Josh said. "Of course, it made me a bit uncomfortable that day, when I found out that our fifty-fifty partnership had suddenly become seventy-thirty. Never figured out how that happened, kiddo."

"The partners' committee voted it. You know that."

"Hey, it's me, Josh—don't bullshit your old partner. I mean, even the paintings in the office that we supposedly owned fifty-fifty. Pretty good stuff. Those paintings were worth twenty million, I later found out. Then I discovered you owned them."

"I personally picked out those pieces. I took a gamble on new artists."

"New artists? I don't think so. Suddenly the press describes you as this great art collector. But it was the agency's art. And mine." Josh took a hit of his new drink. "But you also owned the press, didn't you, Justin? You spoon-fed them. That's how our talent agency, yours and mine, became your agency. And our power, your power. I watched it happen. I couldn't quite figure out the hows and whys, but I knew it was happening."

"Where are you going with this?" Justin glowered. "I mean, we've both moved on. You're the great corporate CEO. Our agency's been broken up. We each have new lives . . ."

"You're right, Justin. We've moved on. I mean, I was going to mention that parcel of land you also managed to slip out from under me. The Malibu property I was about to buy for my new bride. To build her dream house . . ."

"Oh, for God's sake, Josh . . . That was a complete misunderstanding."

"Was it? I wanted that property. I made the mistake of telling you I wanted it."

"You were low-balling the deal, Josh, and you got called on it. If you wanted that land so bad, you shouldn't have done your usual bottom-feeding."

"My offer was strong enough . . ."

"Then why did the realtor start shopping it again? When he came to me, he said Haim Saban had offered almost a million more than you. You'd already lost it. I made an offer 'cause it was on the open market. You know all that."

"No, I don't, Justin. Matter of fact, I checked back with Jerry Post, the realtor. Also with Saban. There was no other offer. You bought it out from under me. And later you sold it at a profit."

"So what's the message here, Josh? If you want to hate me—if that makes you feel good—so be my guest."

"I don't hate you, Justin. I feel sort of sorry for you, but I don't hate you. I mean, I've got a life. A career. Two young kids."

"Listen, I let you play the good guy to my bad guy all those years. I let you be Mister Nice while I played the heavy. When Mel Gibson fired us to go with ICM, it was your idea to pull that shit at Warner Brothers and get his picture canceled. I mean, I did the dirty work, but it was always your idea."

"Sure, I played the good guy. If you'd tried to be the good guy, no one would have believed you. But who gives a shit? We both came away with more money than we ever dreamed about. I used to have nightmares that our clients would find out how much money we were making off them—that they'd fire us on the spot."

"They figured it out a long time ago," Justin said. "Lucky for us, they were also making a shitload of money, so they let us get away with it."

"So we did the job for them. Hurrah for our side." Josh glanced at his watch. "Maybe I'd better get back to the boat . . ."

"It's not a boat. It's a fucking yacht. A gigantic fucking yacht . . ."

"Okay, have it your way. I have a gigantic fucking yacht and you have a gigantic fucking chateau . . ."

Justin caught his breath. "How do you know about my chateau?"

"Just a rumor I heard . . ."

"It's no one's fucking business. Not till I button things up, at least."

"Hey, don't get paranoid on me. I mean, it's a good time to buy a place over here. The old French families, they're looking for cash. Interest rates are low. I mean, I'm looking at a place myself . . ."

"What sort of a place?" Justin asked.

"Nothing spectacular. Just a place for my family, my kids . . ."

"Where's it at?"

"Maybe a few minutes from here. It's seventeenth century. Lots of grounds. My daughter likes to ride . . ."

"Weird coincidence, isn't it? Both of us looking at places."

"What do they say about great minds?" Josh was on his feet. He plunked a fistful of euros on the table for the drinks.

"So this was just a chance meeting, right?" Justin said, still seated.

"I'd heard you were staying here. Thought it would be a gas to surprise you."

"Well, you surprised me."

Josh shrugged and managed a fleeting smile. "So, it's off to the boat . . . I mean, my gigantic fucking yacht." And he was gone.

Justin drained his sambuca. Then he felt himself go suddenly cold. He grabbed his cell phone. His hand was shaking so badly he was having trouble punching the numbers. He heard le Doucet's voice, groggy from sleep.

"This is Justin Braun. I thought you were going to give me an update," he barked.

"Ah, well, you see, the situation . . . it has become somewhat confused. So I thought I would call you tomorrow when things were straightened out."

"I've lost it, haven't I?" Justin choked on his own words.

"As I said, it is confusing . . ."

"Stop bullshitting me, you frog motherfucker. You sold it out from under me, didn't you?"

"I had nothing to do with it. I am serving you faithfully."

"But the chateau?"

"A new bidder has suddenly emerged. Another American. The realtor said he raised the price by one million euros. His provision was that his offer be responded to immediately."

"Fuck . . ."

"There are other places I could show you . . ."

"The buyer's name. It was Litwin, right?"

"I do not know."

"It was Josh Litwin?"

There was a pause. "Oui, monsieur. I am sorry."

Justin Braun pushed "off." He felt himself growing smaller in his chair. So small he felt he had almost disappeared.

Hard Bargain

People have told me that when you're a witness to tragedy, the experience is instantly more surreal than real. It's the shock that distorts perception. At least that's how it seemed when I saw Barry Gal's lifeless body floating half-submerged in his swimming pool. Sure, I felt horror. Barry was my friend and benefactor. He was also a survivor, not a victim. How could this happen to him? What flashed before me was that scene in *Sunset Boulevard*—the writer floating in the pool. Why was that image haunting me now? Barry wasn't a writer. His mansion was on Starlight Terrace, not on Sunset Boulevard, but it, too, was vast and lonely and Barry had ventured dangerously beyond his depth.

And all that mattered now was just one question: What had really happened to him? Why had he drowned? I suppose I knew the answers but I didn't want to deal with them at the time. Not then; not ever.

Of course, I'd had a good run with Barry Gal. Maybe too good to last. Looking back on it now, I've come to realize that when you get involved with a man whose life is shrouded in secrets, you also end up with too many secrets. I'm not happy about that part of it.

I'm basically an open guy. Strangers in bars unload their troubles on me. People tell me I have that sort of peasant Greek mug that says, "trust me." Well, Barry Gal trusted me. Maybe he trusted me too much.

Barry Gal liked to think of himself as a collector. He collected companies and girls. He kept the companies but always dumped the girls. From the first time I met him, I could tell he was a loner. I'd heard he lived in a faux Spanish castle in the Hollywood Hills, complete with tennis court, screening room and the other Hollywood stuff. But no one knew much about Barry—just that he was rich. He had a slight accent that sounded Middle Eastern, but he told girls he was born in France. I figured it was really Lebanon, maybe Algeria. He was a good-looking guy who always wore black jeans and a black leather jacket, and to the wannabe models and actresses who crossed his path, he seemed like a cool guy.

I met Barry five years ago when he opened his first club in Hollywood. I'd been hired to do the walls at one of the private rooms. When I say "do," I mean painting—big frescoes with the usual floating nymphets and succubae. I called myself an artist, but basically I do art-on-demand for tasteless people. So I'm doing these big erotic frescoes for Barry's club and he likes them and asks me to do his screening room at home. I ask him, "You want more of the same?" and he surprises me. "Do whatever you like," he tells me. "Just let it happen." I took him up on it. I've always been a fan of Léger—things like his "Sitting Woman"—so I surprised him with my version of Léger. He flips and I end up not only doing other rooms but also living in the guest house behind his Andalusian castle with this great studio to work in. Suddenly I'm feeling like maybe I'm more than a housepainter.

Living with Barry had its fringe benefits. In addition to collecting companies and girls, he wanted to collect art. I'm no expert in the art market, but we hit the galleries together and I told him what I liked. Before I knew it he was writing checks. He must have gone through a million bucks, but he got some nice pictures for it. He threw a couple of parties at his house for business contacts who admired his collection. He even hung some of my canvases and two of them sold.

Over time Barry opened up to me a little, telling me about his girl friends and business deals and every once in a while a story from his past. He also told me about his chronic back problems and I started helping him out, giving him his daily shot of fentanyl, which is strong stuff. It's a painkiller so powerful it's given only to terminal cancer patients. Barry was a real pill junkie—he had a king-size stash in his medicine chest, but he could never stand jabbing himself with a needle.

The good news was that Barry was on the road half the time on business. When he was gone I had time to paint, but I also became a sort of caretaker, which seemed a fair trade-off. He had a big place and he needed someone to run it, so why not me? Especially since he intended to build a five-thousand-square-foot addition to the main house—a plan that pissed off his neighbors on Starlight Terrace. They didn't want him to shoot movies on their street or to chop down some gorgeous old eucalyptus trees. I could see their point, but Barry couldn't. It got so they didn't talk to Barry, not that he cared.

So one day I get an e-mail that Barry is returning from a three-week trip to Europe. I stock up on provisions and bring in a cleaning crew to tidy up the main house. I sensed that something was in the wind the moment Barry's limo pulled up. Instead of the usual black Lincoln sedan, a long Mercedes stretch rolled through the front gate. When Barry climbed out he wasn't wearing his usual scruffy travel clothes but looked sharp in a blazer and charcoal slacks. Then he extended his hand to Miranda, helping her out of the limo as though he were Cary Grant in a '40s MGM movie. She stood there, squinting in the bright sun, and he said grandly, "Madame, your castle awaits you." She looked dazed as she took in the big house with all its gleaming Moorish tile.

"Well, say something," Barry boomed.

"I . . . I really don't know what to say."

"This is your home, Miranda. Yours and mine. And you know my buddy, Frank Kalamaris. If you continue with your painting, under his guidance, you will be in the hands of a master."

Miranda looked at me and smiled and I saw this stunning little creature, barely five feet tall, with a pert face and short brown hair in a pixie cut. She instantly reminded me of Leslie Caron in those Maurice Chevalier movies, but she's American, perhaps in her late twenties. She seemed excited, yet there was something guarded about her, like she was taking it all in but committing to nothing.

That night, after Miranda turned in, Barry buzzed me on the intercom. "I'm pouring," he said. I met him five minutes later in the paneled bar that looks like it belongs to a London club. "I've lost it," he said. "I can't keep my eyes off her. I can't keep my hands off her. I feel like I'm eighteen, not forty-four. This is a first for me."

"What's not to like?" I said, stunned by his condition.

Barry was already on his second Jack Daniel's. "I want this to work," Barry said. "And I know I'm not good at it. I'm better at sending them away than making them stay."

"Hey, I'm not one to give advice. Two marriages, two divorces. That's a zero batting average." He gave me a nervous grin. "So where'd you find her?" I asked. "In Paris?"

"Sure. She was Arvin's squeeze. Arvin Wright—the guy who saved my butt on that teen movie."

"He saved your butt and you took his girl?"

"He knew he couldn't afford her. He's, you know, the starving artist type. Miranda's got richer tastes."

"Then she chose the right guy. Congratulations, Barry."

"Hey, maybe I've grown up. I mean, there's always that hope."

"Always," I said.

Barry gave me a bear hug. "I'm jet-lagged. Better turn in."

Then he said: "I'm gonna need that fentanyl. Young girls aren't turned on by old guys with bad backs."

Barry never did get around to explaining the business with Arvin and Miranda, but that was all right. I kept my distance the next few days. I'd been working on a big landscape and needed time to focus. Going to my car one day I caught a glimpse of them splashing around in the swimming pool like a couple of kids. Later they were hitting tennis balls.

A week after Miranda's arrival we had a drink together and Barry was all smiles, which amazed me. The Barry I'd gotten to know was a moody guy, if not downright morose. He loved wheeling and dealing, but when things went sour he took it personally. He once told me that he made his money from a chain of dry cleaning establishments, having figured they yielded the best return. Then he started buying limo companies, parking garages, nightclubs and lots of real estate in L.A. and Vegas. As he got richer, he decided to take a flier on a movie company—that way he could introduce himself to girls as a producer, not a dry cleaner. It was a smallish distribution company that specialized in horror and hip-hop pictures—the B-picture sort of thing—but Barry's parties got bigger and the girls prettier, and his name began turning up in the gossip columns.

It was in his new role as a movie maven that Barry crossed paths with Arvin Wright. Barry's company had put up $500,000 for the rights to distribute a little horror film called *Mean Teen*, but what he didn't know was that its director, a hipster who went under the name McT., was strung out on

Ecstasy and lithium. McT. disappeared before Barry could see his cut. It was a classic Hollywood trap. There was no way the movie could be released in its present form. Scenes were missing and you couldn't follow the story.

Barry didn't like being played for a sucker. He got mad— real mad. It was like his Lebanese side took over. He was determined to find someone who could fix his picture, whatever the cost. Finally the young banker type who'd put up the completion bond for *Mean Teen* told him about Arvin Wright. Arvin, he said, was a strange cat who lived in Paris and had an absolute genius for rescuing movies. He'd once been a Hollywood film editor but moved to Paris with the hope of becoming a famous auteur, only it never happened. Meanwhile, he'd become a gun for hire—that is, if you could get him to work. Arvin preferred to hang out in cafés and bullshit with his French friends.

Barry took the next plane to Paris, but when he finally nailed down a meeting with this "auteur," he got exactly what his banker predicted—a flat turndown. Barry haggled and hondled. Arvin still said no. Barry offered to pay him $10,000 if he'd just look at the movie. Arvin softened. After screening it, though, Arvin was grim. He warned that rescuing the project would be tough and expensive, and might even require some reshooting. Barry knew he was being hustled but he raised the ante. In the end, his persistence paid off. A deal was struck—apparently a rich deal, but Barry never told me the details. All he said was that this deal was different from anything he'd ever done.

So Arvin started his surgery on *Mean Teen*, expecting Barry to retreat to Los Angeles, but Barry decided to hang around. He said he was fascinated by the process. More important, he was fascinated by Miranda, who was Arvin's live-in. They would go to clubs as a threesome, with Barry always picking up the tab. As Arvin's working hours continued to stretch, and his deadline loomed, Barry and Miranda became a twosome. Arvin was too absorbed in his rescue mission to do anything about it.

Barry returned to Hollywood for a few days to deal with business problems, and when he returned to Paris I went with him. The new *Mean Teen* was ready. Watching it with Barry in that scuzzy screening room, I couldn't believe it was the same movie. The story worked. The effects were great. Arvin Wright was a goddamn master.

So Barry suddenly had a respectable movie that could go out and make him some money. He had something else, as well. He had gotten Miranda to go to Los Angeles, and everyone seemed amazingly cool about it. As the weeks passed, I expected Miranda to become homesick for her friends in Paris, but she seemed blissed out. Based on past experience, I also expected Barry to start pining for his freedom, but he seemed okay. As for Arvin, he apparently was busy on his next project in Paris and never even checked in. This can't last, I kept telling myself, but I was wrong.

At Christmas, they celebrated their first four months together with a big blast. Barry always acted like Jay Gatsby at his parties. He'd greet his guests, but then he'd sort of hang back and watch. His so-called friends were really people he knew through business. He told me one night he had only two real friends—me and, now, Miranda. He gave a Christmas toast to Miranda that night. "Please join me in wishing Merry Christmas to my love, Miranda," he told his guests. Miranda shot me a quick look. That was the first time either of us had ever heard him use the word "love." And his Christmas gift to her was pure Barry—emerald earrings that lit up the room. The next day they left for a week in Hawaii, returning like a tanned honeymoon couple.

Miranda had started visiting me every afternoon to work on her painting, and we set up our easels side by side. I was worried about Barry's reaction, but he seemed glad that she was taking an interest in something. She was just a beginner, really, but she asked all the right questions and tried hard to improve her technique. Now and then we'd cruise the galleries and talk about the pictures. Miranda had a quiet intensity about her, but kept her feelings very much to herself. She never reminisced about the past. Those times seemed locked away in her mind.

One day as we were wrapping up, I asked her, "Do you ever miss Paris—the cafés, your friends?"

She frowned. "Of course I do. It was a perfect life, but I was very young."

And that was it—a quiet resignation. She had been young in Paris. And now she was living with an older man in Los Angeles and going to bed early and giving him shots of painkiller for his back.

She'd asked me about that, once. "This fentanyl—is it really safe?"

"I wouldn't take it. I mean, how much is too much?"

"What should I do?"

"Barry's a hypochondriac, Miranda. He's healthy, but he always feels he's coming down with something. You know how he is."

The next day Miranda failed to appear for her painting lesson. Instead, Barry put in a rare appearance in my studio. He surveyed the room, pausing at one of Miranda's efforts. "Is she any good?" he asked.

"She's working at it. Rarely misses a day."

"She's in a state today," Barry said. "Her old boyfriend's in the hospital. It's pretty bad."

"Arvin? She never mentions Arvin."

"She was ready to get on a plane today to see him."

"And is she going?"

"I told her to wait a couple days. She can't do anything for him at the moment. Maybe when he goes home . . ."

"She take that okay?"

"No, she didn't." Barry rubbed his chin, like a man pondering his moves.

"Maybe you should let her go then," I said.

"Miranda is pregnant. Has she told you?"

"No. How do you feel about it?"

"Disbelief."

"Maybe it'll settle you down."

"I don't know. I feel that everything in my life is up in the air. That's what a woman can do to you."

The next day we learned that Arvin was dead. When I next

saw Miranda she seemed devastated. "It was pneumonia," Miranda said. "That's the word. I don't understand. He was so healthy . . ."

"Apparently he'd been working eighteen-hour days on his movie," Barry said. "That's what his lawyer told me."

"He always dreamed of making his own movie, not just doing salvage work. And now it's all ended badly," she said.

Barry and Miranda flew to Paris for the funeral and were gone five days. When they returned there seemed to be a distance between them. For the first time I felt uncomfortable with them. They told me little of their trip, and I decided not to ask questions.

One week after their return, however, Miranda appeared at my studio. "Can we take a walk?" she asked. It was a chilly June day and the hills over Starlight were draped in fog. Miranda walked quietly for a time. "Do you know about the screening tonight?" she said finally.

"Barry left me a message that he was showing something . . ."

"That 'something' is Arvin's movie."

"You mean there really is a movie? Arvin actually pulled it together?"

"I am more amazed than you. Arvin was an artist, but not the most practical of men," she said.

"Any idea what it's about? Did he say anything to you?"

"Not really. The last time Arvin and I talked was back in Paris. He had just returned from a long lunch with Barry. Arvin poured some wine and said, 'Miranda, some things just run their course. That's the way it is with you and me. It would be best if we parted company.' "

"That was it? Just out of the blue?"

"Yes, just like that. I was so stupid, I said, 'What will I do? Where will I go?' And he said, 'Find someone who can take care of you. Someone like Barry Gal. Yes, it should be Barry.' "

"Like, he willed you to Barry?"

"And when I packed my things and was ready to leave, Barry was there. He was waiting. And Arvin said to me, 'I know you will understand some day.' Those were the last words we exchanged."

"And you went with Barry . . ."

"We'd been seeing each other. We were comfortable together. We were not lovers, or anything. I was in shock and I became so passive . . ."

Miranda walked on ahead of me now. I let her walk alone.

That night, when Miranda and I entered the screening room, there were twelve others in the room. I sat in the last row and Miranda nestled in next to me. After everyone was seated, Barry walked to the front. "Thanks for coming, everyone," he said in a voice that seemed a little shaky. "The movie you're going to see was created by my friend Arvin Wright. Some of you guys knew of him and his work. He was very talented, but he's gone from us now and his movie remains. It is a very personal film that he wrote and directed. As you know, Arvin was a perfectionist, so he would be pissed at me if he knew I was showing his work when it's still not in a polished state. It has a temporary score and it has to be redubbed—why am I telling you this? You're all pros and are used to seeing films in this state. Because this is so different from anything I have ever experienced, however, I need your advice. You understand marketing and distribution. So I guess what I'm asking you is, would you guys try to take this movie to the public? How would you market it? This is Arvin Wright's legacy and I want to do right by him. Thank you for coming."

With that Barry signaled the projectionist, the room went dark and the movie began. I could feel Miranda's body tense as the film unfolded. Barry was right. It was a love story—a very unique, passionate movie. I'd never seen anything remotely like it. The movie itself was jumpy, the story sometimes hard to follow, and the actors certainly weren't Redford and Streep. But the audience was riveted and so was I. No one stirred. Toward the last ten minutes I even saw people dabbing their eyes.

As the movie drew to a close, Miranda bolted from the theater. The lights came on and Barry was quickly surrounded by his guests, heaping praise on him. "It's not exactly an Eddie Murphy comedy, but it'll do business," said one rough-looking guy. "I'd take it to the Cannes Festival. I mean, it's downbeat as hell—the sort of stuff they love over there."

"The guy who directed it . . . he really died?" someone asked.

Barry nodded. "This was his story. His and the girl's."

"So that gives you a helluva marketing campaign. You could exploit the shit out of the dead lover angle. I can see *Access Hollywood* going for that big-time. Even *20/20*."

I'd heard enough. I had to find Miranda. I looked along the dark paths behind the house for several minutes before I finally came upon her standing in the shadows, staring into the swimming pool. She did not look up as I approached.

"The son of a bitch."

"I don't know what to say, Miranda."

"So Barry bought me. It's all in the movie. He bought me from Arvin."

"There obviously was some sort of a deal between them . . ."

"And the deal was that Arvin would get to make his movie. And he chose to make his movie about me. About us."

"Look, Miranda, I am Barry's friend."

"And your friend thinks he owns me, so he is now going to exploit me still further by showing this movie . . ."

"I'm sure Barry didn't know what the movie was about. How could he know that Arvin was obsessed with you?"

"Stop it. They made a deal, those two . . ."

"Businessmen make deals. Only this one was a killer deal. It killed Arvin."

Miranda's eyes were blazing. "And Barry? Does he deserve any better? He should meet the same fate as Arvin. That's what he deserves."

She was staring directly into my eyes. Tears rolling down her face, she darted off into the darkness.

And the next morning, I was staring at Barry's body in the pool, not believing what I was seeing, not accepting that any of this could have happened. I was paralyzed. I couldn't get myself to call 911. I couldn't get myself to touch his body. I couldn't get myself to call Miranda. First I had to sort out that, yes, this was real, Barry was dead, and I was standing there confronting this surreal reality, and what it all meant.

Of course, I finally made the call. The police came promptly and did their work. There was, however, no formal police investigation into Barry's drowning. The autopsy revealed a massive overdose of fentanyl, which was deemed to be self-administered, since the needle and the medication were beside his bed. Miranda was questioned for less than fifteen minutes and tearfully told the police of her alarm over Barry's excessive self-medication. A day later, she packed her things.

I offered to drive her to the airport. She said she preferred to go alone. "I am returning to Paris," she said. "It is the only place I've been happy."

"What can I say, Miranda?"

"I know you were Barry's friend, but you've also been a true friend to me," she said. "I know there were things you could have told . . ."

"But to what end?"

"His shots . . . You knew I gave him his shots . . ."

"I don't want to know, Miranda."

She started to leave, then turned and we embraced. Then she was gone.

There was no funeral. Barry's will, I soon learned, left the house to Miranda, who remained in Paris to have their baby. It also provided that I should live in the studio as long as I wanted. The will also designated that a healthy share of the profits from Arvin's movie would go to Miranda. I knew this would ultimately be a substantial sum, since the film, titled *Hard Bargain*, went on to win awards on the festival circuit. Arvin was even selected for a posthumous "best new director" award at the Montreal Festival. The movie ended up doing quite well for an art film, both in the United States and overseas.

Barry would have been pleased by all this, of course. The irony was that, in the end, we were all enriched by knowing Barry Gal. He was a winner. But he was also a man who lived with too many secrets; even in his death there were too many secrets.

But those are the trade-offs, I suppose. I mean, life is a series of trade-offs. And along with the deals comes the baggage.

The Neighbors III

The June meeting of the Starlight Terrace Neighborhood Association was held at Elizabeth Donahue's home, a rambling Cape Cod whose green shutters urgently needed a coat of paint and whose front lawn was a battlefield of weeds and crabgrass. "Thank you all for coming," Eric Hoffman began. "I thought it best to move the meeting ahead a week in view of these recent events."

"For a change we have something to dish about," Sidney Garman said.

"I'm still in shock," Nancy Mendoza put in. "None of us liked this man, or his movies, but I never thought it would end like this."

"It's a scene out of *Sunset Boulevard*," Marty Gellis said. "I mean, drowning in his own pool."

"According to the police, Barry Gal's drowning stemmed from an overdose of a painkiller," Eric Hoffman said. "That's the official police version. He self-administered the drug, then fell into the pool."

"I don't buy this *Sunset Boulevard* crap," Sidney Garman said. "People don't drown in their own pool. Especially if there's a girlfriend there and also this painter guy . . ."

"Life may not always follow the logic of your screenplays," said Nancy Mendoza.

"There must be another element," said Elizabeth Donahue. "Perhaps the girlfriend was carrying on with the painter. Something like that."

"I was carrying on with the painter, remember?" Denise Turley reminded. "Trust me, he's not the type to shove some-one into a pool."

"The dark secrets of Starlight Terrace, emerging at last," said Tom Patch. "It's a fucking movie of the week."

"I hate to inject business into this discussion," Eric Hoffman said. "But there's the issue of the lawsuit. Barry Gal's attorneys filed their response. It's all pending."

"With Barry gone, why go to the expense?" said Nancy Mendoza.

"Those bulldozers are still poised to strike," said Hoffman. "We know nothing about the position of his heirs."

"You have nothing to worry about with the heirs." The voice belonged to Frank Kalamaris, who had slipped into the room and quietly taken a seat to one side.

"Well, if it's not the mystery guest," Denise Turley said. "How they hanging?"

Frank Kalamaris smiled at her. "I apologize for intruding.

I know this is a private meeting. My name is Frank Kalamaris and I lived with Barry and there were some things I'd hoped I could clarify. . . ."

"Everyone knows who you are," Denise Turley said.

"I'd like to extend my condolences," Eric Hoffman said.

"Thank you for that," Kalamaris said. "Look, I realize Barry was not very popular in the neighborhood. But Barry was a good man. And he was truly upset by your lawsuit."

"So what will happen with the property?" Nancy Mendoza asked.

"Barry's will is clear," Kalamaris said. "The house goes to Miranda, who will soon be the mother of his child. Miranda wants to live in Paris but she's decided to keep the house. Perhaps their child someday will want to return. In any case, the house was leased to Mr. and Mrs. Justin Braun. According to Barry's wishes, I will continue to live in the studio behind the property. And plans to expand the house have been abandoned."

"In that case, you've saved us all a lawsuit," Hoffman said.

"To show her good faith, Miranda has offered to pay the association's legal bills. She regrets the whole situation."

"That's very gracious," Elizabeth Donahue said.

Kalamaris was on his feet now. "So that's what I came to tell you. Unless there are further questions . . ."

"The police . . ." Sidney Garman said. "They found this drug in his system, but . . ."

"I'm afraid I can't shed any light on that. The police questioned me. They questioned Miranda."

"How'd he fall into the pool?" asked Marty Gellis.

"I suppose people fall into pools if they're on drugs," said Kalamaris. "Barry was into strong stuff like fentanyl. It helped him with his back pain. It's all very tragic."

"Don't take this the wrong way, Frank, but do you think . . . Well, were there any signs Barry was suicidal?" asked Sidney Garman.

"He had a lot to live for."

"That begs the question."

"But I'm afraid I'm out of answers." Kalamaris turned and walked slowly to the door.

"He seems like a straight shooter," Eric Hoffman said, after he was gone.

"I think he's sexy as hell," Denise Turley said.

"So first Todd Plover turns out to be gay. Then Barry Gal turns out to be dead. Never a dull moment around ol' Starlight," Sidney Garman said.

"Let's go home before another shoe drops," Denise Turley said.

"So moved," said Nancy Mendoza.

"People don't just fall into swimming pools," said Marty Gellis.

"We've adjourned," said Eric Hoffman.

And with that the directors of the Starlight Terrace Neighborhood Association filed from the room and trudged home over the bumps and potholes.